Manhattan Is Missing

By the same author:

Lemon Kelly
Jim Starling and the Colonel

Manhattan
Is Missing

by E. W. Hildick

Illustrated by Jan Palmer

Doubleday & Company, Inc., Garden City, New York

To

Betty Kronsky and Ritzi

(who started it all)

Library of Congress Catalog Card Number 68–22475
Copyright © 1969 by E. W. Hildick
All Rights Reserved
Printed in the United States of America
First Edition

Contents

1

Boy Meets Cat

"You'll be sure to look after Manhattan properly, won't you?"

Mr. Cape had his hat in his hand, ready to go. At least it looked as if he was ready to go. But he'd been standing there like that for the past fifteen minutes, ever since the Clarkes had arrived, and some of them were beginning to wonder if he was changing his mind about letting them have his apartment.

Mr. Clarke smiled nervously. He took off his glasses and put them on again.

"Why of course we'll look after it properly. We'll look after it as carefully as if we were the New York City Council and it were the *real* Manhattan."

"Hm!"

Mr. Cape didn't look very impressed. Tall, dark, anxious—he went on standing there with his hat in his hand, slowly turning it around by the brim. He was looking at them out of narrow eyes, with his head on one side.

"Manhattan the *place*, you know," said Mr. Clarke, explaining his joke.

"I know," said Mr. Cape, glumly, still standing, turning, looking.

"We thought it was ever such a good idea," said

Mrs. Clarke, pausing on her way to the kitchen. "Naming a cat after the part of the city in which you live."

"We're thinking of renaming ours when we get back to London," said Peter Clarke. The boy was cradling Manhattan in his arms, gently stroking his cheek against her whiskers. "Chelsea. After the part *we* live in."

"Good job we don't live in South Kensington, that's all. What a mouthful! Imagine calling out 'Here, South Kensington, South Kensington, South Kensington' every time you wanted him to come indoors!"

The last speaker was Adam. He was tall for a sixteen-year-old—taller than his father—and the purple-and-yellow-striped pants he wore made him look taller still. He was bending over Mr. Cape's phonograph records, his long hair falling forward over his ears. He hadn't bothered to turn around and Mr. Cape—whose face had brightened a little at the reminder of Peter's obvious love for animals—was looking darkly anxious again.

"I didn't name her Manhattan," he said. "She was already named when I bought her."

"Ours is called Smoky," said Peter. "He's all gray. Well—a blue-gray. With bits of white here and there."

"Siamese are different from ordinary cats. You know that, don't you?"

Mr. Cape looked as if he'd made up his mind to concentrate on Peter: to focus the whole of his anxiety on the twelve-year-old boy.

"*Smoky* isn't an ordinary cat," said the boy.

He'd been tickling Manhattan under the chin and

looking into her eyes. He had a theory that if you looked into a cat's eyes long enough—three minutes at the very least—without either of you looking away, that cat would be your friend for life. But this was something that had to be settled right away and he turned and stared up at Mr. Cape.

"Smoky—"

"Sure, sure!" The man was smiling now. "I guess for you there's no cat like Smoky, is there? Well that's how it is with Manhattan and me. You *will* take care of her?"

"Don't worry, Mr. Cape," said the boy, turning back to his inspection of the cat's blue eyes. "Look how she's settled already."

"Peter's very good with animals," added Mrs. Clarke, who'd had a glimpse of Mr. Cape's kitchen, with its dishwasher and big refrigerator, and was now more eager than ever to make sure he didn't change his mind.

"Siamese are very nervous, you know," said Mr. Cape.

"She's settled now, anyway," said Peter, staring, green into blue, fancying he could hear the first ripple of a purr.

"They get jumpy. Unexpectedly. You have to watch for that. They—"

"HEY!"

It was as if the yell had been meant to test Mr. Cape's words.

Mrs. Clarke gave a little scream, Mr. Clarke dashed to the window, Mr. Cape nearly dropped his hat, and the cat sprang out of Peter's arms and into the kitchen. Even Adam had been made to straighten up. Then he shrugged and grinned.

"Benjie," he said, with a hairy toss of his head toward the balcony.

"You're coming in and you're staying in! Until we've unpacked."

Mr. Clarke sounded grim.

"But I want to stay out here. Look! All lit up. Coming up the river."

"Benjie's seen a boat," said Adam, turning back to the record cabinet. "He's just spent the last five days on one of the biggest liners in the world. He's only been on dry land a couple of hours. And now he's doing his nut over a bit of a river boat!"

"Mum! Peter! Come and look—"

"Inside!"

With an extra tug, Mr. Clarke pulled his youngest son into the apartment. Benjie was like his mother and Adam. Dark and thin, with large brown eyes, he was almost as tall as Peter, even though he was three years younger.

"Adam, it's all lit up and there's a band on it, I can hear it, it—"

"It's someone's radio you can hear, you nit!"

"Don't you call me a nit!"

Benjie's dark eyebrows came down and a small white fist flew up into Adam's back.

"Here!"

Adam had gone lurching forward into the record cabinet.

"Benjie, behave yourself!" roared Mr. Clarke.

"The voyage—they've been so cramped—they're not usually—" began Mrs. Clarke.

But Mr. Cape wasn't there to listen to her excuses. He was on his hands and knees in the kitchen with Peter, trying to coax Manhattan from the depths of a cupboard under the counter.

"You see what I mean?" he grunted.

"I think I can reach her."

"Well be careful, then. . . ."

Peter fumbled around until he felt the cat's ears. Then he began to scratch between them.

"Come on, then . . . it's all right now . . ." he murmured. "Only my idiot brother . . . he won't harm you . . . come on then . . . *that's* a good little cat. . . ."

Mr. Cape stood up and sighed heavily. He brushed his knees with his hat.

"As I was saying . . ."

Oddly enough, it looked as if Benjie's yell had helped to settle his mind. It looked as if all that had been needed to reassure him was the sight of Peter in action in some small emergency.

But with a man as anxious as he, you can never be sure from one minute to the next. Especially with a family like the Clarkes around. And, of course, a cat like Manhattan . . .

2

The Two Manhattans

With Manhattan safely back in Peter's arms, Mr. Cape went on with his warnings and instructions. The cat was jumpy, they'd all seen that. (Here Mr. Clarke nodded and gave his youngest son a sharp prod on the shoulder.) Manhattan was very highly strung and liable to run for cover at any sudden noise. ("Poor thing!" murmured Mrs. Clarke, shaking her head sadly.) But that was only natural with Siamese, continued Mr. Cape, with a harsher note in his voice and a frown for the interrupter. It hadn't anything to do with the way the cat had been brought up. ("Good heavens, I'm sure it hasn't!" said Mrs. Clarke.)

"Apart from that nervousness," continued Mr. Cape, addressing Peter once more, "she shouldn't give you any trouble. So long as you feed her correctly."

"Yes, sir," said Peter, pressing an ear against the cat's warm neck. "Only don't you think she's a bit on the fat side?"

"No," said Mr. Cape. "I don't. Or at least I don't mind if she is. There's to be no dieting her, do you understand?"

"Hoh!" laughed Mr. Clarke. "We'll diet *him* if he tries it!"

His sudden barked laugh had caused Manhattan to struggle in Peter's arms. Mr. Cape was not amused.

"That's all right," murmured Peter, making the same reassurance do for both the cat and her master.

The cat responded by struggling less violently, but Mr. Cape's hat was twisted around at a faster rate than ever.

"You promise?"

"I promise," said Peter.

"You'll follow the instructions on the note I've left? Exactly?"

"Exactly. Three quarters of a can every morning and the rest of it last thing at night. With a few of those biscuit things."

The hat's revolutions slowed down.

"And fresh water."

"Yes, sir. It's probably not the amount of food anyway. It's probably that she needs more exercise."

"*No!*"

Manhattan jumped again. Peter had to let her go. She leaped down and went under the table, shoulders hunched in two bristling lumps, eyes wide, tail slowly sweeping.

Benjie laughed.

"That wasn't me this time. That was *you!*"

Mr. Clarke slapped his pointing finger, but Mr. Cape wasn't taking any notice.

"I'm—sorry," he said, partly to the cat, partly to the crouching, coaxing Peter. "But I must make it clear that there's to be no attempt made to exercise her down there." He nodded toward the window. "It's tempting, I know. And I've often thought about taking her into the park myself. But you see how busy it is . . ."

The Clarkes looked down at the strip of lamplit grass and trees that ran between the apartment building and the river. The street outside the building was busy enough, but beyond the grass, at the side of the river, there was a broad expressway, with a roaring stream of cars running in either direction.

"A blowout, a squeal of brakes, the blare of a horn . . . No," said Mr. Cape. "She'd just take off and run. And there aren't any kitchen counters for her to run under down there."

"She might jump into the river," said Benjie. "Can she swim? Cats usually can."

"Benjamin . . ." murmured his mother.

The boy was looking too eagerly interested in the idea for comfort.

"She'd never reach the river," said Mr. Cape. "Those cars are traveling at around fifty, you know. And there aren't many gaps between them."

"Yes, but cats have nine—"

"Benjie!"

"Dad?"

"Shut up! Go out and watch the boats."

"Gee, thanks, Dad!"

"'Gee'? Where on earth has he picked up *that* expression?" growled Mr. Clarke, looking at his wife as if she'd been responsible. "He's only been in the country five minutes."

"Three hours and five minutes," said Adam, going

over to the telephone corner and thumbing through the directory. "And don't forget it was an American ship. . . . Do you mind if I make a call, Mr. Cape? There was a girl on the ship who lives in Brooklyn. Should be home by now."

"Go ahead, go ahead," muttered Mr. Cape. "So long as you pay for what you use that's all right by me. . . . But about this exercise question," he went on, fixing Peter with his narrow eyes. "Taking Manhattan out *is* out. O-U-T. Understand?"

Peter nodded. He was smiling. The cat had come out from under the table and was standing, with one small but heavy pad, on the middle two toes of his right foot. His cat. Plonk!

"I wasn't thinking of taking her out, sir. I was thinking of games in here. You know—bits of string and that, sir."

Mr. Cape seemed relieved to hear it. Even cheered. "I guess that's O.K.," he said. "I guess she *doesn't* get enough of that sort of exercise. The cleaner's kid sometimes plays with her . . . But watch the ornaments, huh?"

"They'll watch the ornaments!" growled Mr. Clarke, glaring at his sons in turn. "I can assure you of *that*, Mr. Cape. And since we're responsible for any damage, you can be sure that if there *should* be an accident—"

"Well, O.K. But that vase there is worth four hundred dollars, for example."

"Oh dear!" sighed Mrs. Clarke.

"And that stool in the corner . . ."

Peter was relieved to find that Mr. Cape had other

worries. He'd suddenly begun to feel rather tired of being the focus of the man's anxious attention. He picked up the cat and scratched her gently under the chin, while his parents and Adam discussed the contents of the apartment with the owner, reassuring him and inquiring about such details as how the air conditioner worked and what sort of soap to use in the dishwasher and where was the rejector switch on the record player and how often the cleaning woman came. With Manhattan in his arms, the other Manhattan—the place, the island on the Hudson River, the heart of New York City—began to slide into his thoughts again, just as it had seemed to slide there as he stood on the deck of the ship with all the others, watching the lights in the steadily looming buildings. . . .

The ship was late. It was growing dark as they approached the pier. Everyone was excited. Even his father had gotten over his anger at having had to be corrected about the bridge.

"We're just going under Brooklyn Bridge, boys," he had said, gazing up at the huge arching span of lights. "Isn't it a marvelous sight?"

"It would be if it *was* Brooklyn Bridge," Adam had said, winking at the girl he'd made friends with. "But it happens to be the—er—"

"The Verrazano-Narrows Bridge."

The girl had laughed. Julie, her name was. . . .

"Is Julie home yet?"

Adam was trying to telephone her now. Peter

thought he could hear the hum of the telephone re-
ceiver, and then realized it was nothing of the sort.
It was Manhattan—the cat Manhattan—purring, rum-
bling rich and deep against his face. He closed his
eyes and held her tighter and, outside, down below
—where she must never be allowed to go—the other
Manhattan rumbled too: a low, deep roar of cars, taxis,
buses, with the wail of a siren beginning to thread its
way nearer, a silvery thread of sound. . . .

Like a Christmas tree, it had looked, Manhattan
against the clear, pale evening sky as the boat edged
closer. Like a *forest* of Christmas trees, all lit up.
That's what his mother had said, squeezing his
shoulder.

"Look, Peter—Benjie—look! Isn't it lovely? Just like
Christmas trees."

Benjie had asked her what she was crying for then.
And wasn't it a bit silly, he'd asked, all this talk of
Christmas when it was only July—and *so* hot?

"They're all burning coffee by the smell of it," he'd
added. "Sniff up! . . . Yergh!"

Sure enough, there had been a sort of coffee smell,
but it wasn't as unpleasant as Benjie had made out.
Anyway, Benjie was a fool. *He'd* rather have gone
to Brighton again for his holidays—and why? Because
the last time they'd been there, a year ago, he'd found
a shilling on the beach. He believed that if they kept
on going there he'd find more shillings.

"He'll have to be satisfied with dimes now," Peter

said, half to himself and half to the cat. "Nickels, dimes, quarters, and dollars," he murmured.

And dollars reminded him of the ship's band, blaring out brassily as the gangway was made ready. "Hello, Dolly!" they were playing, and then the workmen, dockers—stevedores, didn't they call them here? —came on board with the band still playing, and one of them, a big fat man with a red shirt, had done a kind of ballet dance on his toes with one finger on his bald head all around the ship's baggagemaster, who looked as if he could have clapped him in irons.

"We're gonna like it here," Adam had then said, laughing.

"We're *going* to like it here," his father had corrected him. "Especially if we remember to stick to our mother tongue."

"They say 'gonna' in London too," grumbled Adam. "We're gonna like it here—if you lay off the nagging."

He'd said the last bit very quietly though. . . .

"Yes. We certainly are. We're going to like it here," said Mr. Clarke, shaking Mr. Cape by the hand. "And don't you worry. Everything's going to be properly looked after. The cat's in excellent hands, as you can see."

"She's purring for me!"

Mr. Cape's eyes were still narrow as he looked down at Peter. But this time there was a warmer, more confident gleam in them.

"Yes," he said. "I guess you're right."

Then, with a scratch for Manhattan and a fist for

Peter—which he knocked gently against the boy's chin in a gesture that could have been one of trust—he left for his holiday in France.

Or was it a final warning, wondered Peter, rubbing the place where the cold, hard knuckles had brushed his skin. He tightened his hold on Manhattan as she gave a little tug toward the door through which her master had gone.

3

Mr. Clarke Lays Down the Law

"Right!" said Mr. Clarke, when the soft clash of the elevator doors told them that Mr. Cape was on his way at last. "Right, my lads! I've one or two things to say to you. Benjie, come on in this minute, at once . . . *Benjie!*"

"Aw, Dad, you said I could watch the boats and—"

"In! And don't stand there with the door open. You're letting all the hot air in."

"Huh!" grunted Adam. "There'll be some hot air to let *out* before long."

"What's that?" snapped Mr. Clarke, giving his right-hand mustache a brisk tug.

"Oh, nothing!" sighed Adam. "Where d'you want us?"

He knew the signs. They all knew the signs. The barked "Right!" The tug at the mustache. The glares from side to side. Their father was going to lay down the law.

Usually, back home in Chelsea, he ordered them into his studio for this. There he would sweep aside the litter of sketches, rough book-jacket designs or whatever else he'd been working on at the long, paint-and ink-stained table, pick up his longest brush and proceed to wag it at them.

"This table will do," said Mr. Clarke now, waving toward Mr. Cape's highly polished round table in the dining corner of the room. "Get yourselves a chair apiece."

"Don't you think it's a bit late, darling?"

Mrs. Clarke was looking pale and tired. Her shoulders were drooping and her chin and neck had a sagging look.

"Late in the day, yes," said Mr. Clarke. "But early in the campaign. And the earlier in the campaign the better. You go and have a lie-down if you want. It's this lot I want words with. . . . Peter, put that blasted cat down and get yourself a chair. Benjie, I shan't tell you again. Adam, if you *dare* pick up that phone before I've done, I'll wrap it round your neck!"

Sighing, grunting, scowling—they made their various ways in their various manners to the table.

"Right!" said Mr. Clarke, suddenly sounding sweetly reasonable—still crisp but not angry. "There are one or two things I want you to get firmly fixed in your heads."

Before he had started working for himself as a book illustrator, he'd been a teacher. As Adam used to say (privately), during these sessions their father went right back to nature again.

"First of all," began Mr. Clarke, "I want to remind you of the purpose of the exercise. *You've* come here on holiday—to enjoy yourselves—*and take that silly smirk off your face, Adam!* . . . Yes . . . *you're* on holiday. But your mother and I are here on business.

The only holiday *we're* getting is on the boat coming over and on the boat going back. So I want you to remember that and make a special effort to help."

"But what can we—?"

Mr. Clarke cut Adam short.

"You can help by keeping out of mischief. All of you. And being prepared to look after yourselves a bit. Your mother and I will be out much of the day during the week. For a couple of hours after breakfast we'll be in, probably, arranging appointments and things like that. We want to see as many people here as possible in the next four weeks—editors, publishers, agents, and so forth. Many days we'll not be in for lunch. That's another thing you'll have to be prepared for—seeing that you eat the food your mother will get ready for you. In a civil manner. At the proper time. And without squabbling—"

"But what if we don't like it?"

"Benjie . . ." Mr. Clarke leaned forward and tapped his youngest son on the nose. "You *will* like it. And if I hear of any grizzling from *you* when we get home, you'll be in trouble. Is that clear?"

Benjie scowled up through his dark fringe of hair. "Yes, but—"

A harder tap on the nose.

"Clear?"

With an indignant jerking of the shoulders, Benjie said harshly: "Clea-*yurrr!*"

Mr. Clarke gave his mustache a tug and went on: "You're tired tonight, I know. We're all tired. But I must say, chaps, your behavior in front of Mr. Cape left a lot to be desired. Adam, you conducted yourself like a lout. You slouched around the flat as if you were thinking of burgling it. No wonder the man was all jumpy."

"Just because of my hair and my clothes. It's not fair the way—"

"That's enough!"

"Well it—"

"That's *enough!*" Mr. Clarke thumped the table. The boys sighed, rolled their eyes, groaned—according to their habit. All were thinking the same thing, though. That they might as well have been back in that studio in Chelsea for all the difference it made, being in New York. Skyscrapers, sirens . . . what was going on around didn't seem to matter. Home was a well-thumped table.

"I don't care if you grow your hair down to your ankles and wear your mother's petticoats—"

"Heh! heh!" cackled Benjie.

"You belt up!" snarled Adam.

"You can wear what you *like*, lad—but you're to conduct yourself like a civilized human being or I'll want to know why!"

"Darling, don't you think it *is* rather too late—"

Mrs. Clarke had stuck her head around the kitchen door. Her husband waved it back.

"I've nearly finished," he said. He turned back to the boys. "So there it is. You'll be on your own much of the time. But there's plenty to do in the vicinity. I've no objection to you young 'uns going over into

the park there, for instance, or up to the shops round
the corner—"

"The shops round the corner!" groaned Adam.
"What a swinging holiday this is going to be! Anyway, they call them *stores* over here."

Surprisingly, Mr. Clarke didn't get mad. He smiled
instead.

"The *shops* round the corner happen to be on Broadway, my boy. Just think of *that*."

"Yer, but—"

Adam broke off and shrugged. As he pointed out
to the others later, what was the good of trying to
explain to such "an old perfectly right-angled square
as Dad" that Broadway was a long, long street, changing its character every ten blocks or so. "He seems to
think it's *all* like in *Guys and Dolls*," he had muttered.

"And Adam," continued Mr. Clarke, "I know you'll
want to be out and about a lot, but during the day,
while your mother and I are—"

"That's O.K., Dad," said Adam. "So long as I can
have the evenings and you don't start fussing if I'm not
home by ten."

"Well . . ." Mr. Clarke was frowning. But nodding,
too. Bargains were bargains, after all. "We'll see . . .
yes . . . so long as you're not out *all* night. . . . I
suppose . . . Anyway, the daytime's what we're discussing now. During it, you, Adam, will not stray *too*
far from your post, and will not make *too* many telephone calls . . . nor, for that matter, one or two long
ones, lasting hours. Right? . . . Right! And you, Benjie,
you will do as your brothers tell you, and keep away

from the water over there, and do nothing silly out
on the balcony—understand?"

Benjie gave his head a shake, his eyelids drooping,
nearly asleep.

"As for you, Peter . . ."

Mr. Clarke studied Peter with some perplexity. In
many ways it was unfair telling Peter to behave himself properly. He always did. With Peter it was the
things around him that misbehaved. He was the
dreamy kind and things seem to take advantage of
dreamy kinds. Low tables loaded with fine old china
cups and saucers have a nasty knack of sidling into
the paths of boys who are dreamers. Things borrowed
by dreamers—whether they're one's father's best com-
passes or an elder brother's latest Stones record—
have a habit of breaking or getting scratched on precisely such occasions. Babies being wheeled out by
dreamy kinds seem to put out invisible anchors from
their carriages and so contrive to be left, forgotten,
at the side of playing fields. Dogs taken for walks . . .

At the thought of animals and Peter's failings, Mr.
Clarke gave a little shudder. He remembered the cat.
Manhattan was a very important animal in all their
lives. If they hadn't been prepared to look after her,
there wouldn't have been the big reduction in the rent
of the apartment, and they certainly couldn't have
afforded the full amount. At the same time, if anything did happen to her . . .

Mr. Clarke shuddered again. He was just about to
remind Peter of his responsibility and the need for

vigilance, when a series of loud screams made them all jump up from the table.

"Help me! Quick! Help!"

The screams came from the kitchen.

They were being made by Mrs. Clarke.

4

Manhattan on Guard

They rushed to the kitchen door.

Then stopped short.

"Good heavens, Jean, what on earth are you playing at?" said Mr. Clarke.

"Playing nothing!" cried his wife. "Get her off me!"

She was on her hands and knees in front of one of the cupboards under the sink. Peter recognized it, from the cans he could see through the partly open door, as the place where Manhattan's food was kept. But he didn't spend much time inspecting the cans. As with his father and brothers, his eyes were drawn to Manhattan.

For there sat the cat, her tail neatly tucked around her haunches, plumb in the middle of Mrs. Clarke's back. Her eyes were slowly widening and closing, widening and closing, as she gazed back at the man and boys—as peaceful and placid as if she were sunning herself on a yard wall. Mrs. Clarke's screams didn't seem to have startled her a bit.

"Look, don't stand gaping! Everytime I move she digs her claws in to stop herself from slipping. Lift her off!"

Peter stepped forward and did as his mother asked. Manhattan was purring.

"Well I'm blowed!" said Mr. Clarke. "What a daft thing to do. Are you all right?"

"How d'you mean—'What a daft thing to do'?"

Mrs. Clarke stood up, fumbling gingerly at her back.

"Kneeling down and putting the cat on your back. What d'you expect?"

"I *didn't* put her on my back! She jumped on. I was just looking into this cupboard and she jumped on my back. I wondered what on earth it was."

"So did we," laughed Benjie. "*I* thought you'd been electrocuted."

"What's so funny about that, then?" snapped his father. "You think it's a joke if your mother gets—?"

"Oh, leave him alone, Bruce!" Mrs. Clarke was thinly smiling now. "I suppose it did look funny. What I want to know though is what she did it for."

"Instinct," said Adam.

"Eh? How do *you* know?" asked his father. "It's the first time I've heard of a cat jumping on people's backs."

"I know," said Adam, "because it was in the manuscript of that book you had to illustrate—*Cats in My Life.*"

"I don't remember anything about—"

"No, Dad. That's because you didn't read it all the way through. You never do."

"Now look here—if you think you can do my job better than I, you'd better—"

"Bruce, you know very well what Adam's saying is true. I'm always telling you the same thing . . . But go on, Adam. This instinct you were talking about."

Adam shrugged.

"Well, it's only a theory, but they do say that Siamese cats were originally trained as guards. Temple guards. Back in Siam. They used to sit on the lintels over the doors. They must have been pretty small doors because the idea was that if any thief or trespasser came through—stooping, you know, with his back bent—*kerlump!* He'd get a cat on his back."

They all stared at Manhattan. She stared back—placid still, still slowly blinking her eyes—from Peter's arms.

"Well I must say it makes sense," said Mrs. Clarke. "I know if I'd been a burglar, I'd have let out such a yell it would have woken up every priest in the temple."

"And it looks as if her instinct warned her to expect a yell, too," said Mr. Clarke. "I mean she didn't go jumping off and under the table this time, did she? . . . Benjie—no!"

But he was too late.

Benjie had bent down just in front of Peter.

"Me a temple thief!" he gibbered, in what he apparently meant to be a sinister Siamese tone.

And out of Peter's arms wriggled Manhattan, and on to Benjie's back.

"See?" said Benjie. "It's worked again, heh! heh!"

Peter reached out to relieve him of his watchful burden, but his father put out a hand and winked.

"Leave her there," he said. "He asked for it."

Benjie tried to straighten up. Manhattan, still looking very placid, dug in a little. Dug in a *lot,* by the sound of Benjie's yell—but then he always had been one for crying before he was hurt.

"Take her off me!"

"Come, boys. Lets go back in the other room."

"So long, Benj!"

"See that he doesn't get away, Manhattan."

"Aw, please!" cried Benjie. "Ouch!"

"You'll just have to keep very still, my boy," said Mr. Clarke. "You know, dear," he said to his wife, "I think we ought to get one apiece for them. Three Siamese cats. Keep 'em pinned down. We'd know where they were, then. . . ."

But after a few seconds, Mrs. Clarke slipped back and freed the Temple Thief.

It was quite a big apartment, with a separate bedroom for the boys. Normally, this held only one bed, in a corner of the room opposite the door—a recess with a dressing table, mirror, electric outlet, and an extension telephone. Adam, of course, had been quick to claim this as his corner and to follow it up with a battery of threats about what he'd do to Peter and Benjie if they dared trespass there.

But the two younger boys weren't a bit bothered really. Naturally, Benjie had had to test Adam's threats by going straight over and jumping on his brother's bed. And naturally Peter had had to present Adam with a string of what-ifs. What if the phone rang and Adam wasn't there? What if the cat ran under Adam's bed and wouldn't come out? What if a burglar came into the apartment, while Adam was out, and tried to steal the silver-framed photograph of Ann Marie, Adam's best girl back in Chelsea, or the leather-bound address book in which he'd written the name and telephone number of Julie, who looked like being his best girl here in New York?

To the jump on the bed Adam had responded with a clip on the ear—thus satisfying Benjie's curiosity. To the string of what-ifs he'd replied with an elaborate chain of in-that-cases that had set Peter's head spinning and made him wish he'd never raised the subject.

But, having made their protests and stated their misgivings, Benjie and Peter were quite happy to let Adam have his corner. After all, the other two beds were much better placed, one on either side of the long window, with a view of the Hudson River that stretched from the last of the big piers down on the left to the George Washington Bridge far up on the right. . . .

Peter lay half sitting against the pillows for a long time that night, staring out through the slats of the Venetian blind at the lights twinkling on the bridge, and listening to the continuing roar of the traffic on the expressway below. Benjie, who had also spent some time staring out, had fallen asleep in the sliding ruins of his kneeling position, face downward in the pillow with his backside in the air. ("A bit like a sinking ship really," thought Peter.) As for Adam, in the soft glow of the reading lamp he'd claimed as his own, he was still slowly turning the pages of a magazine he'd found in the apartment—one that told what was happening that week in New York, what shows, films, trips . . .

Peter wriggled further down the bed and closed his eyes. He wasn't interested in shows and things and couldn't understand Adam's interest. There were shows and things in London, weren't there? Why come all this way to waste your time on shows? And what right had Adam to jeer at Benjie and his ships when he was just the same himself over shows and groups and things?

Now cats—that was different. Adam would probably say, "What about you, then—wasting so much time on this Manhattan? You might just as well have stayed home looking after Smoky instead of getting Mrs. Ellis next door to do it." And Peter would have had several answers to that. One would have been that it was a

good job someone *was* prepared to look after Manhattan. And another would have been that cats are like
people—no two are alike and every single one of them
is worth getting to know. Yet another answer would
have been that when you have a job to do like looking after a cat—and seeing that she doesn't do this or
eat that—you get to know a place better. You *have*
to. You have to know the layout of her home, for a
start: who the neighbors are, whether they have any
dogs that might be at war with her, or any cats of
their own she might like to visit, things like that.
And, in the case of Manhattan, possible bolt holes:
places she might run to if she managed to slip out
of the apartment. Wasn't there a laundry room? And
a place where you dumped your rubbish? And no
doubt there'd be emergency steps, in case the lift
should go out of order. "I mean the *elevator*," Peter
reminded himself, opening his eyes and blinking
around the strange room, now in a bluey-gray darkness, with Adam breathing slowly and heavily, asleep
already.

Peter closed his eyes again. Tomorrow, he thought,
tomorrow I must make sure about all these places—
just in case. And I must—

He stopped thinking about what he would do the
next day and listened. He'd heard a soft, heavy clump
and a faint creak. It could have been Adam, turning
in his bed, or his mother or father, moving about in
the next room. But Peter sensed it wasn't anything of
that sort. And no . . . He had turned to the bedroom
door, where a faint strip of light could now be seen,

all down one side. It was from there that the noise had come.

He smiled in the darkness.

"Come on, then," he whispered.

There came another clump and the strip of light widened. Peter was now staring at its base, at the shadow there.

"That's a good cat!" he whispered, glad that he'd had the idea of leaving the door unfastened when he'd returned from the bathroom.

But Manhattan didn't make straight for his bed, as Peter was hoping. For a long time she sat there, just inside the door, a darker shadow, plump, compact. Then she had a wash. The boy could guess this from the vague movements and the faint harsh gasps. Then, with many a pause for further lickings, she made her tour of inspection—sniffing at slippers, suitcases half unpacked, the magazine that Adam had let slide to the floor, Benjie's socks . . . It seemed to take her hours to get around to Peter's corner and by then he was almost asleep. In fact he was so far gone that the thump on his chest startled him a little.

"Eh! What? . . . Oh, it's *you*. . . ."

Two pointed shadows moved twitching toward his face. He caught a gleam of large round eyes. A wet, cold nose touched the tip of his own. Then the cat turned around—once, twice—still on his chest and softly, steadily kneading into the bedclothes with her paws—three times.

Peter lay still and closed his eyes again. His day was complete. And, as the cat settled to sleep, so he settled. Ships, bridges, towers, taxis, rivers, ships again, the sea, the sea, and shadows . . . His mind slid, slowly spinning, over them all, high above them, back over the waters, and back, back, back to a place that wasn't London, wasn't anywhere he knew, a place of shadows, and doors, and deeper shadows above the doors: small, compact, watchful shadows, with pointed ears cupped forward, listening, on guard.

And—did Peter really dream this or was it something he fancied he'd dreamed, looking back later on what was to happen?—even then, coming toward the shadowed doorways with their sentinel cats, a dark stooping figure was already making its furtive way. . . .

5

Manhattan's Letter

"Remember—you may go out if you wish, but only into the park over there."

"You'll find the sandwiches in the refrigerator. Three separate lots of them wrapped in foil."

"And Adam—remember what I said about the telephone bill."

"There's a fruit cake too—but I want to see at least half of it when we get back."

"We should be fairly early today—about five o'clock."

"Have as many apples as you want—up to three each."

"And don't forget to keep an eye on that cat."

"The doorman this morning is called Franz. If you get into difficulties of any sort, call him on this speaking thing. He knows about you and he's going to tell Chico, the doorman who'll be on this afternoon."

Thus Mr. and Mrs. Clarke finally left the apartment at ten o'clock the following morning.

"Wow!" gasped Adam. "They get worse! . . . I'm just going back to the bedroom, make a phone call. See you don't disturb me."

"That's all right," said Peter. "Come on, Manhattan. I'll give you a grooming."

Taking care to keep a hand firmly over the cat's

shoulders while he bent down to the cupboard in the kitchen, he took out the plastic bowl containing brushes and a comb. She squirmed at the very sight of these articles, making a deep-throated sound that was half wail and half growl.

"You know what these are for, don't you?" said the boy, recognizing the sound as one of pleased anticipation. "I bet old Capers doesn't brush you as regularly as I'm going to."

He decided to do it on the balcony, where there were some canvas chairs and it wouldn't matter about the bits of fur. Manhattan brushed bulkily against his legs at every step, yowling with eagerness.

"All *right,* all *right,*" murmured Peter.

Benjie was already out there, leaning on the railings, looking down. Almost opposite the building was a mooring place for smaller boats: cabin cruisers and the like.

"Wish we'd come to live in one of those," he said, without turning around. "We could have sailed here in it. All the way from Chelsea. We could have done it all on water."

"Don't you lean over so far, that's all," said Peter.

"You tell *her* that."

Benjie pointed to the cat.

"You should have seen her a few minutes ago," he continued. "She sticks her neck through the railings and stares down at the cars and the people. I think she thinks they're beetles and mice or something. D'you think she'll jump one of these days?"

"What? From twelve stories up? Cats aren't stupid, you know."

"Yes, but if she gets excited she might, mightn't she, if she saw what she thought was a *special* mouse?"

Peter stared down. It was rather a frightening thought. Of course, a falling cat—or person—might clutch at one of the balcony railings below, in passing. But still . . .

"She's lived here four years, Mr. Cape told us. And she hasn't done it yet."

"There's always a first time."

"Benjie—sometimes you sound just like Mum. Stop worrying. And anyway, look—Manhattan isn't leaning out now."

This was true. The cat was jumping on and off the nearest chair, prowling around Peter's legs, jumping up again, and stretching out her head to the bowl of brushes.

Peter took the hint. Using the wire brush first, he began briskly but carefully to brush the cat's back.

"They don't like to be stroked backwards," said Benjie.

"That's all you know."

"What's she yowling for then?"

"Pleasure."

"Pleasure! As if anyone likes having their hair brushed."

"Belt up, before I start on you."

"You wouldn't dare—*yeeow!*"

"*That* wasn't a cry of pleasure, I'll admit."

Peter dodged the kick that Benjie had aimed at

him. He lifted the brush again. His brother dodged into the doorway.

"I'm gonna tell now!"

"I should. You go and tell Adam. While he's on the phone. See what you get."

"Adam nothing! I'm gonna put it in a book. I'm gonna make a list for when Daddy and Mummy get back. Adam told me to do it and he gave me a notebook."

"The rat!" growled Peter—though not without a touch of admiration for his older brother's lazy cunning.

"I'll book that down too," said Benjie. "And show it to Adam when he's finished phoning."

"They spell it r-a-t," said Peter, calmly getting on with Manhattan's grooming.

"And I'll write and tell Mrs. Ellis to tell Smoky you're making more fuss of this cat than *him.*"

"You're going to be busy," was all that Peter replied to that.

But it gave him an idea. He'd been meaning to write to Mrs. Ellis himself. He'd forgotten to warn her that although Smoky preferred liver slightly cooked, she mustn't overdo it or it would constipate him. Well, now—what he'd do would be to write a letter as if it came from Manhattan. From Manhattan to Smoky.

"I hope you can spell," he said, giving the Siamese a final smoothing down with his sweaty hands.

It was not a very big balcony—just a strip of concrete with white railings around the edges and an

extra panel of thick red glass along the front. There
was just room for four of the canvas chairs, a rather
sooty evergreen shrub in a large pot, and a small iron
table.

But it was pleasant out there, sitting in the warm
moist air, high above the morning traffic, with a cat
on your lap and a letter pad over the cat. True, it
became rather awkward when the cat stretched her
neck up to see what the scratching above her was all
about. "But after all," Peter told himself, "she *is* sup-

posed to be writing this letter. And these twitches
and scribbles she keeps making me do can be counted
as her own genuine writing."

At this point he paused for a moment, wondering
what it would turn out like if he simply held the pen
to the pad and let the cat bump it this way and
that. Maybe it would cause a real message to be
created, like spirit messages.

Or maybe not, he decided, as the cat gave a particularly lively jerk and caused him to scrawl a line
across what he had already written.

Eventually, after many such pauses, he completed
the letter. It read:

> Dear Smoky, My name is Manhattan and I'm
> the cat the Clarkes are looking after. I am a
> Siamese and I jump on people's backs. I am
> a bit fussier than you about food but that's
> mainly because my owner Mr. Cape is such
> an old fusspot, but I do see your point about
> not having liver too well done, it bungs you
> up, so. I hope Mrs. Ellis remembers not to
> cook your liver too much. The Clarkes are not
> a bad lot really. Peter is the best of course,
> EASILY the most handsomest and kindest.
> Adam is a bit of a wet and Benjie is a bit
> of a nit but they're all right in a way I sup-
> pose, yes, sometimes. Mr. Clarke makes me
> laugh, he fusses just like my owner only not
> as miserable with it and Mrs. Clarke is sweet

enough mostly only she can be a bit sharp
at times. But Peter is definitely, abslutely the
best and he sends you his love and so do I.

Yours sincerely,

Manhattan Cape

Peter studied the signature thoughtfully. He'd tried
to make it look catlike and oriental at the same time
by making little spikes stick out at the corners of the
letters. Then he realized what was missing:

"Come on," he said, lifting Manhattan off his lap
and making her dabble her front paws in the sooty
soil in the shrub's pot. "Now then, lady, sign right
here."

He pressed one of the paws against the foot of the
letter and the result wasn't bad: rather smudged but
obviously a pad print. "Just look!" he said, turning to
Manhattan.

But the cat was displeased. She sat on the floor of the balcony with her back to Peter. Then, after a disdainful lick at one of the rudely treated paws, she stalked to the railings and stuck her neck out.

Peter joined her. He didn't attempt to pick her up and make amends. With cats, such behavior was merely adding insult to injury, he knew. Instead, he leaned against the railings and looked down himself—to the busy street below, with its cars and yellow taxis and a cream and green police car which looked funny from the top, with two brown elbows sticking out at either side from short-sleeved navy-blue shirts, as if inside there was one enormously broad policeman filling the whole front seat instead of two medium ones. Then he looked over on Manhattan's side and saw she was watching a group of people on the crossing: a man in a straw hat, a nurse pushing a baby carriage, an elderly woman with a large dog on a leash, a Great Dane. They were going over to Riverside Park, to the paths among the trees, where now there came a policeman on horseback. Some children were playing on the grass behind him, and two women were sitting on canvas chairs, knitting. Or no. Correction, thought Peter. *One* was knitting. The other was opening a large basket on her knee, lifting the lid. A picnic basket, was it?

Peter was just thinking that it was rather early in the day to be having a picnic lunch—it wasn't eleven yet—when something leaped gracefully out of the basket and on to the second lady's lap. It was a cat! A white cat!

He watched as intently as ever Manhattan had watched the people and traffic below. Now the cat was on the grass. It was sniffing the grass in front of the women, happy in the sunlight, its tail in the air, straight up, with a small kink at the tip.

It didn't seem to be scared of the noise of the cars. True, it might have been used to going there every day. But wasn't Manhattan used to the noise herself? *Better* used to it probably, hearing the roar from her balcony every day—morning, afternoon, evening, night —for four years.

Peter looked down at her: at the eager straining neck and the slowly sweeping tail.

Mice nothing! She knew just as well as anyone else that those were people down there, strolling about, enjoying their freedom, satisfying their curiosity. People and dogs—and cats.

He frowned. He'd have to think about it. But if proper precautions were taken . . .

He sat down again. He picked up the writing pad. Then he wrote, next to the paw mark at the bottom:

P.S. Peter thinks there might just be a chance that he'll take me for a little walk in the park later today.

6

The Very Special Top-Secret Mission

In New York's Metropolitan Museum, not very far from Mr. Cape's apartment, there is a famous statue called *The Thinker*. It is the statue of a man, seated and leaning forward, resting his chin on one hand, and staring intently at the ground a few yards ahead of him. Some such attitude as that is the one most people have for doing their heavy thinking: sitting still, staring into space, resting their chins, or maybe scratching their heads from time to time.

Peter Clarke wasn't one of these.

He wasn't one of those who can't do their deep thinking without a pencil and paper, either.

He was one of the small number of people who can't think about something deeply and in detail, unless they're moving about and doing other things.

And the project that he had in mind for Manhattan's outing on the grass certainly needed thinking about deeply and in detail.

So, for the next few hours, he busied himself in and around the apartment: seeing that Manhattan's bathroom tray of kitty litter was tidied up properly; making toys for the cat out of string and bits of paper (and finding a few old ones, chewed and tattered, that Mr. Cape or, more likely, the cleaner's boy had made for her); allowing Benjie to join him in these activities, and their subsequent trials on the cat, in return for the erasure of Peter's name from the younger boy's Complaints Book; purloining a couple of the lunchtime apples for himself and Benjie without Adam's knowing; having lunch itself; and grandly giving Adam permission to go out for an hour or so afterward (i.e., promising not to tell their parents about this).

During this period—while Peter's fingers were busy with paper, string, apples, tuna sandwiches, and more apples—the plan steadily took shape and the details were settled. Manhattan would have to be taken down to the park in a container like the white cat's, that was for sure. But there was no need for a specially made box, as Peter had at first thought. While searching for a suitable carton—which he did while looking for materials for the cat's toys—he'd come across a real cat basket in the cleaning cupboard. It was dusty and, when he'd taken it out, Manhattan had shown little interest in it—which suggested that Mr. Cape had only got it in case of an emergency, such as if she'd to be taken to the veterinarian's. Peter took care to do much of the testing of her new toys around the basket—getting her to chase the paper mice and birds in and over it—so that she should be used to it when the time came for her trip.

A much bigger problem was that of the lead and collar. Right from the start, Peter had decided that these would be necessary—at least for the first ten minutes or so, until they were sure she wouldn't run away. At the same time, he knew that a rough, string collar, which might cut into Manhattan's neck, would never do. String would be all right for the lead itself, but there just had to be a proper collar—broad enough not to cut, strong enough not to break—to attach the string to.

This took up another hour's active thought after lunch, during which time Peter and Benjie (who still didn't know what his brother was cooking up, or indeed suspect that he was cooking up anything special at all) explored the apartment building and its various possibilities.

First, at Benjie's insistence, they experimented with the peephole on the apartment door, through which the owner could inspect any caller without being seen himself. They took it in turns to go outside, ring the bell, and then twist or flatten themselves into positions from which they couldn't be seen. Then they did it all over again, allowing themselves to be seen, but trying to conceal imaginary weapons, with which they hoped to take the owner by surprise, after luring him into opening the door.

It was a stupid game really, thought Peter—because since the weapons were imaginary anyway, it was hardly a difficult task to conceal them. However, he might as well humor his brother, he decided. He would probably need Benjie's co-operation later and certainly his good will—and, anyway, he himself was still busy with the collar problem. Might he have to go out and buy one in the end? And, if so, how much would it cost? And would one of those shops his father mentioned—those *stores* on Broadway—stock cat collars? Surely there was a good enough substitute, if only he could think of it.

Thinking harder, he played harder, explored harder. To the delighted Benjie, his brother was in one of his good moods, full of bright ideas. How was he to know that those bright ideas were created so quickly and abundantly because they were by-products of a less successful struggle to produce a bigger idea—like sparks coming off a blacksmith's anvil? So they explored the twelfth floor, being burglars in the washroom, spies in the room with the garbage chute (opening the door of the chute and tapping out code messages to an agent five floors below), and firemen wearing breathing apparatus on the emergency steps. (*Faulty* apparatus in Benjie's case, causing him to have to be carried down to the next floor draped around Peter's shoulders.)

Next, they investigated the elevator. On the way down, Benjie remembered that it was televised and shown on a screen in the lobby—so that the doorman could see if anyone was being attacked.

"You attack me," said Benjie, "and we'll see if it works."

Peter felt a stab of alarm.

"What, and have the doorman call the police?"

He knew there wasn't much chance of the doorman doing any such thing. Rather would there be a report to their parents when they came back. But when someone is contemplating a highly risky project like Peter's, he doesn't want it gummed up by attracting attention to minor misdeeds.

"It would be like getting caught speeding on your way to steal the crown jewels," he said.

"What's that got to do with it?" asked Benjie.

"Oh nothing . . . Forget it," said Peter. "I was thinking of something else."

All this activity wasn't wasted, however. It wasn't only something to do while Peter was fixing the details of his Plan. All the time they were fooling around, Peter kept his eyes open. One problem would be to get Manhattan out of and back into the apartment without anyone's knowing, apart from Benjie. Adam was taken care of. The "hour" he said he'd only be gone for would be more like three or four, if Peter knew anything about his elder brother. Probably he'd be strolling in a mere ten minutes or so ahead of their mother and father. But Adam was only one hazard. People in other apartments mustn't know either. And, most important of all, the doorman mustn't get wind of it. Peter had a strong suspicion that Mr. Cape would have asked the doormen to keep a special watch on all activities concerning the cat.

So—to test the doorman's vigilance—Peter grandly allowed Benjie to do a little fooling in front of the television camera.

"No fighting, mind!" he warned. "But sing a song or something, wave, make faces—go *on!* It's up there in the ceiling."

Faced with such a direct order, Benjie went all bashful. It took three rides up and down before he'd perform.

"O.K., baby," the doorman greeted him, when they stepped out into the lobby. "Who ya think y'are? Johnny Carson?"

This must be Chico, thought Peter, smiling back at the tall dark man in the light-blue uniform. He'd never heard of Johnny Carson, but he guessed he must be some television performer. He also guessed that this Chico must have a pretty sharp eye.

This was confirmed immediately.

"You got stage fright or something?" he said, still grinning at Benjie. "It took ya three trips before you'd do anything. Three takes, just for *that!*"

"Sorry!" whispered Benjie.

"That's O.K., baby," said Chico. "It's a quiet time just now. Only don't you go taking joy rides when it's busy, will ya?"

"No, sir," said Peter.

Chico looked at him.

"You're the English kids, aincher? Up in the Cape apartment? . . . Yeah . . . You ever see the Queen? Queen of England?"

"Twice," said Peter.

"Three times," said Benjie. "Once she came past our school when he had the measles."

"Did she now?" said Chico. "Well did you ever see her at one of these command performances?"

"Only on television," said Peter.

Chico chuckled.

"I got a cousin who's a dancer who danced at one of your Queen's command performances. How about that?"

Dancers weren't very high on either boy's list of impressive people. But Peter put on a courteously interested face.

"Fine," he said.

"Well now," said Chico, "I'm gonna ask you to give me a command performance. On my own network: RMS. The Riverside Mansions System."

He waved at the battery of blue-white screens on the wall of the lobby.

"You're allowed one performance a week. Each. And it's gotta be good. So you rehearse it, see? You think up an act and polish it nice. Then you give the performance. None of this ad-lib trash. O.K.?"

It was such an engaging idea that Peter almost forgot about the Plan.

"You mean on here?"

Chico nodded.

"One two-way trip—up and down—each. At a quiet time. Remembering we're not wired for sound. It has to be pantomime. And I'll watch."

They agreed. Benjie was all for working out an act there and then, but Peter plucked his sleeve. Chico's last word had been like the last piece of a jigsaw puzzle and the Plan was now complete.

They'd use a wrist watch for Manhattan's collar. It would be perfect.

Peter was already taking his off as they stepped into the elevator, on their way up.

"Benjie," he said, "forget about this TV act thing for the time being. I'm going on a very special top-secret mission. Want to come?"

7

"Catch Her—Quick!"

For all his love of animals, Peter didn't know much
about cat collars. He'd seen plenty of cats wearing
collars and had always assumed that they took to
them as readily as dogs seemed to take to theirs. He
hadn't realized that those cats he'd seen had had to
be trained to wear collars—and that this training had
had to be conducted very carefully and very tactfully
when they were still kittens.

About ten minutes after he and Benjie had re-en-
tered the apartment, wrist watch at the ready, that
gap in Peter's knowledge had been filled. The watch
lay on the floor, in a corner, behind the television
set, where it had been tossed by Manhattan at the
third attempt to get it around her neck. She herself
sat crouching all a-prickle under the table, glaring out
at the boys. And Peter and Benjie sat on the rug
facing her, sucking at the scratches on their hands and
arms.

"Maybe it's the ticking that did it," said Benjie.
"Maybe if we gave your watch a bash and stopped
it."

Peter shook his head.

"Probably stopped already," he said. "Anyway, it

wasn't the sound. It was the feel of it. Collars and leads are out."

"What shall we use then?"

Peter shrugged.

"We'll just have to keep hold of her, that's all. Or be ready to grab her and put her back in the basket. Hovering over her. You know."

Benjie looked pleased.

"We're still gonna try it then?"

"Sure we are."

Peter grimly munched at one of the deeper scratches on his forearm. He wasn't a willful boy, but when, after careful thought, he'd set his mind on something, he didn't easily give up—no matter what the snags.

"Right!" said Benjie. "Let's go then."

He stretched out to pick up the cat. Peter pulled him back.

"Don't be stupid! We'll have to wait till she's calmed down."

"She *is* calmed down."

"She isn't. Look at that bristly ridge along her back. We might have to wait until tomorrow now."

Benjie shook off his brother's arm.

"Oh no we're not!"

"We might have to—idiot!"

"We won't!"

"I'm in charge of this."

"You're *not* then! We're partners. You said so coming up in the lift. You said if one gets into bother the other will, too. Partners . . . And anyway, we needn't let her out of the basket. Just this first time,

we can just take her over there and back without letting her out. Get her used to being carried about."

Peter frowned again. There were times when Benjie
made good sense. He felt almost angry with himself
for not having thought of this before. But even if they
didn't let her out of the basket on the first trip,
wouldn't it still be better to wait until the following
day? She was still looking bristly around the neck.

Benjie seemed to read his thoughts.

"If you don't do it today, this afternoon, now," he
said, "you won't do it at all."

"Huh? How do you—?"

"Because I'll tell, that's why." Benjie got up and
clumped to the writing desk for his Complaints Book.
"I'll tell them what you're thinking of doing."

Peter sighed. When Benjie set *his* mind on something, he too didn't give up easily. At the same time,
Peter wasn't as furious as he might ordinarily have
been. He'd already been wondering how he himself
could possibly last out until the next day before going
ahead with the Plan. The next day, after all, might
not be so convenient. There might be rain. Or a high
wind. Or Adam might take it into his head to hang
around the apartment.

Today it was warm and sunny and calm. The coast
was clear—completely Adam-free.

"O.K.," said Peter. "But she's to stay in the basket.
And we don't start till she's a bit more settled. Maybe
if we gave her some cream she might—"

"Good idea!"

Benjie was already in the kitchen, opening the re-frigerator door, and causing Manhattan's ears to twitch in a promisingly normal way.

Twenty minutes later, the boys were over in the park, screened by trees from the apartment building. The basket lay between them.

"She didn't mind a bit!" said Benjie, peering through the cracks, delighted.

"Good cat!" said Peter.

"It just shows," said Benjie.

"What?" asked Peter.

"That you want to take more notice of *me*. This was my idea."

"You! *You'd* have gone straight past Chico with it, mate! You'd have gone with it bang under his nose instead of waiting till he'd gone to open the taxi door for that lady. So you can wrap up!"

"We-e-ll . . . So what? If he'd asked what it was, I was ready. I'd have said it was a picnic."

"Huh! And maybe he'd have believed you, too!" grunted Peter.

He was happy, though. To him it seemed perfectly obvious from Manhattan's silence that she was finding the new experience a pleasant and interesting one. The smells alone must have fascinated her. He plucked a handful of grass and slipped it through the crack between the lid and the body of the basket. Manhattan gave an ear-flapping shake of her head, then sniffed at the particles of green stuff. They watched, smiling, through the cracks.

"She's still a bit bristly," said Peter.

"Yes, but not half as much as when we were messing about with the watch round her neck. What a stupid idea!"

Peter didn't reply. Very carefully, he was lifting the lid a little. Then he slipped a hand through the aperture and rubbed Manhattan's chin and neck.

"I suppose we *could* bring her out just for half a minute or so," he murmured. "Just to let her have a good look round. Keeping tight hold of her, I mean."

"Ooh yes! Me first!"

"You not at all! Not today. Tomorrow maybe. But not today. I must do the holding today."

"I'll tell!"

"Tell away then."

There are some occasions when you simply have to brave a young brother's blackmail. And there are some occasions when a young brother knows it's not going to work.

"All right," said Benjie. "You hold her. I'll hold her tomorrow. . . . Go on then! What are you waiting for?"

Peter was looking around carefully, watchful for dogs, listening for possible frightening noises that might rise above the regular rushing of the traffic up on the street and over on the expressway.

It seemed peaceful enough. Behind them, on the path, some young women were walking along pushing baby carriages. A little girl, trotting at the side of one of the carriages, was laughing, slapping at a bunch of toy balloons that hung from the hood of the carriage. Some elderly women were sitting on a bench a little farther along the path, chatting in loud but not alarming voices. A man lay stretched out on the grass a few yards away, his straw hat tipped over his face, softly snoring. From somewhere beyond the trees came the slow clopping of a horse's hoofs—a pleasant sound.

Gently, carefully, firmly, Peter got a flat-handed grip on Manhattan's sides. Slowly he lifted her from the basket. Then, transferring one hand to the top of her breast, just under the chin, and sliding the other back to support her haunches, he cradled her firmly to his chest.

"Keep that lid open," he murmured, gently but urgently.

"She's purring!" said Benjie.

Peter smiled, almost purring himself, as Manhattan gazed around, wide eyed.

"There's a good cat," he murmured. "Just a quick look round. Then we'll take you back home. But tomorrow we'll—what?—"

It sounded just as if someone had fired a gun. A woman screamed. A child wailed. The straw hat fell from the face of the snorer. And, with one jerk, Manhattan was out of Peter's hands and scampering across the grass.

"Catch her—*quick!*" he cried.

8

Manhattan Besieged

The noise was only that of a balloon bursting. Or maybe two of them together. Peter saw this—saw the women bending over the little girl, now bawling with her head thrown back—saw a few colored shreds of rubber at her feet. But it was only in a flash, out of his eye corners. He was already running hard, crouching forward, after the chocolate-pointed, golden streak that was Manhattan.

Luckily, she was heading straight along the grass, parallel to the path, making neither for the street up on the left nor the expressway on the right.

Yet.

"Stop her!" cried Peter, trying to attract the attention of the people farther along the path and those who were sitting or lying on the grass. "Stop that cat!"

They turned, or sat up and twisted around, staring at Peter and the equally frantic Benjie.

"What'sa matter, son?" someone asked.

"Hey! Look where you're going!" another shouted, as Peter leaped over a prone body, nearly upsetting a bottle of sun-tan lotion.

"That cat!" cried Peter. "Stop it! . . . Manhattan!"

"Manhattan!" cried Benjie.

Maybe they shouldn't have shouted at all. They only seemed to be making the cat go faster. And certainly they shouldn't have shouted her name. Peter realized that afterward. It was only drawing people's attention to *them,* the boys. And this was not surprising really, with a name like that, the name of the place. Back in London, Peter and Benjie would have stared themselves if they'd seen two strange boys tearing along and bawling out "Chelsea!"

"They're nuts!" someone said.

"Manhattan!"

"English nuts, by the sound."

"Stop her, *please!*"

It was a dog who obliged first. A large, rather plump, golden retriever who'd been placidly ambling along the path. Seeing this small animal, golden like himself, dashing toward him, caused him to stop. Then he trotted forward with a bark.

It might have been a friendly bark. It probably was. But Manhattan was apparently taking no chances.

She slowed down, crouching, almost crawling, ears back, bristling. Then she veered, picked up speed, and went hurtling along toward the street.

"Oh, *no!*" cried Peter, who'd managed to get within a couple of yards of her swishing tail.

It was not as bad as if she'd swerved toward the expressway, but bad enough.

"Stop her!"

By now, some people were beginning to see what all the fuss was about. A boy with dark glasses and two girls in mini skirts converged on the cat as she crossed the path. Another dog joined in, a small black one, yapping, running across the grass on the streetside of the path. Once again Manhattan veered. An old man snatched off his hat and tried to bar her flight with it. Then—with a jump and a series of scratching, slithering jerks—Manhattan ran up a tree.

"Well . . ." gasped Peter. "It's better . . . better . . . than the road."

"There she is!" said Benjie, pointing up to where Manhattan sat crouching, flanks heaving, ears back, on one of the lower limbs. It was about fifteen feet up, far too high to reach.

"You stay by the trunk," Peter ordered Benjie. "I'll try to coax her down."

"I can climb up and—"

"No! She'll only go higher. Remember that time when Smoky was a kitten. You stay by the trunk."

He turned back to Manhattan.

"That's a good cat, there's a good cat then," he said, soothingly.

But Manhattan's eyes flashed wildly from face to face below her. Already a crowd had gathered and this wasn't helping Peter one bit.

"Good cat, then! It's all right!"

But he was having to shout to make himself heard above the crowd, and it wasn't easy to sound calm and reassuring.

"Look!" he appealed to the onlookers. "Please be quiet. She'll never come down if you don't."

"'S a free country, son," said a man in a straw

hat, chewing a cigar. "We can talk if we want to. You English?"

"You heard what the kid said," chipped in another man in a straw hat. "Leave him get the cat down nice and quiet."

"So now we got spare-time policemen in the park, huh?" said the cigar chewer, glaring at the other man. "Where's ya badge, feller?"

"Look, please, both of you," said Peter. "All I'm asking—"

"All he's asking is for you to keep ya big mouth shut for two, t'ree seconds, buster, that's all," the second man said to the cigar chewer.

"And so what if I don't wanner, feller?"

For all their threatening words, the two men didn't really look as if they were going to come to blows. It seemed to Peter as if they were enjoying themselves, as if it was simply their own contribution to a lively scene, put on for the entertainment of the crowd. But it wasn't helping him at all.

"There's a good cat," he said, cocking an anxious eye up at the still crouching, still wildly staring Manhattan.

"You sure gonna get into trouble now," came a voice from behind Peter.

He turned to find a boy of about his own age, though fatter and with shorter, fairer hair, and wearing glasses, staring up at the cat.

"That Mr. Cape's cat?" said the newcomer, without taking his eyes off the animal.

"Yes," said Peter. "How do you know?"

"I live in the same building. Lower down. 5E. You're English, aren't you?"

"Yes, but—"

"Ever been in Scotland Yard?"

"Lots of times. But just now—"

"Just now you're busy. So I see. I'd climb up and get her for you if I didn't have these new pants on."

"No thanks. I mean thanks all the same. Only that would make her go farther up."

The boy shrugged.

"It's *your* problem. See you."

And he strolled off, with a last glance up at the cat.

"Hey! Wait—"

Peter had wanted to ask him to keep quiet about what he'd seen, but the boy was already somewhere behind the crowd.

Peter turned to Benjie.

"Fetch the basket," he said. "I'll keep an eye on the trunk. . . ." He bent back his head. "Come on!" he wheedled, wriggling his fingers, and moving his arm away from Manhattan toward the trunk.

The cat seemed to have him focused by now, but she still remained crouching, bristling, conscious of the crowd, besieged.

"Aw, come on, Manhattan. . . ."

"Manhattan?" said a woman, giggling. "What a crazy name for a cat!"

"What's crazy about the name of Manhattan, lady?" asked the cigar-chewing man. "You want for it to be called The Bronx or Yonkers or somep'n?"

"The lady was only making a polite remark," said the other straw-hatted man.

"Ar right! So I was only making a polite reply," said the cigar chewer. "Ainchoo gone back to City Hall to collect that badge yet?"

"Talking of badges, mister—"

"All right, all right! What goes on?"

The crowd turned, parted, then reassembled behind the policeman on horseback. Now everyone seemed to be talking.

"You," said the policeman, looking down at Peter. "This your cat?" he said, looking up at Manhattan.

"Yes, sir—officer. I mean it's not actually mine, but we're looking after it, yes."

The policeman's jaw relaxed.

"You English?"

"Yes, officer."

"You know Liverpool?"

"Well, not really."

"I got a cousin there. . . ." The policeman looked up at the cat and stretched up an arm. But even he was too far down.

"I—I think I'd better have a go at climbing up, after all," said Peter, noticing that Benjie was back with the basket.

He moved toward the trunk.

"Oh no you don't, son," said the policeman.

"But I've tried—"

"Let the kid go up if he wants!" came the voice of the cigar-chewing man.

"Do what the sergeant says, officer!" jeered the other straw hat.

The crowd began to buzz again.

The officer took no notice.

"You stay right down there," he said to Peter.

"But why can't I?"

"Because it's not allowed in the city parks, that's one thing. And if you fell off and broke your neck, I'd be in trouble for sitting here letting you. You an alien and all."

"He's right!" said a woman.

"Well *you* go up then, copper!" said someone else.

Then the comments came in a rush.

"Send for Mayor Lindsay!"

"Whyn't you fire your gun over its head?"

"Call the fire chief!"

Still the policeman took no notice. He took a stick from his belt and reached up with that. It just scraped a leaf a few inches below Manhattan. The cat bunched herself tighter.

"Police brutality!" jeered someone in the crowd.

"Hey, feller!" said the cigar chewer. "Let the kid stand on your shoulders. . . . I mean that," he added. "No kidding." And he took out his cigar to prove it.

The policeman looked as if he'd spent a lifetime ignoring the advice of men in straw hats.

"You'll just have to wait till she's ready," he said to Peter. "She'll be down when she's hungry."

"Hey, feller! I made a suggestion. Why don't you let him stand on your shoulders?"

This time the policeman did flick him a glance.

"Why don't you just mind your own business, daddy?" he said.

"*I* know . . ."

Peter turned to see Benjie at his side, looking all eager for the first time in the past fifteen minutes.

"You know how she jumps on backs, how she can't resist it? Well then, let's get down and see."

Without a word, Peter went down into a crouch, next to the horse, under the cat, with Benjie crouching at his side.

A howl came from the cigar chewer.

"Ya don't have to *bow* to the cops, you guys! It's still a free country. Take his number if he don't let you go up and git the cat—don't *bow* to him!"

"Daddy," said the policeman, "I'm warning you . . ."

"It's no use," said Peter, turning his head sideways and looking up with one eye.

"We're too far down," said Benjie.

"If only we were up there," muttered Peter. "On his horse. We—*hey!*" He straightened up, pulling Benjie with him. "I've had an idea."

"What? Jump on the horse behind him?"

"No, you nit! Listen . . ."

As Peter whispered in his ear, Benjie giggled—and it wasn't because his brother's breath was tickling him.

"Now do it properly," said Peter. "Keep your voice down. And get ready for when she jumps. *If* she jumps . . ."

Benjie played the part perfectly. He walked around to the front of the horse and waited politely until the policeman had finished what he was saying to the cigar man. Then he looked up.

"Sir," he said. "There's something very important about that cat—about who it belongs to—it's ub opp ib nupp . . ." Benjie continued in a mumble.

"What? What's that, son? Speak up!"

"It belongs to a bubbu de siddy cowble ub it op . . ."

"*What?*"

The policeman bent toward the mumbling Benjie.

Peter looked up.

Manhattan was staring down, wide eyed.

She would never have a broader back than that, thought Peter, crossing his fingers tight.

And—plump!—even as he did so, down jumped Manhattan, causing the crowd to gasp, then shout.

Peter hadn't known exactly what would happen next. He'd had some vague idea of bending forward himself, presenting a second back, a second tempting step down. But he needn't have worried.

The reflexes of a New York City policeman are rather quicker than those of an average British housewife or a young lad like Benjie. And the skin on his back is infinitely tougher.

So there was no squealing or screaming or pleas for the cat to be taken off. Before Manhattan or the crowd knew exactly what was happening, up jerked the navy-blue back and around it came a huge brown hand.

"Gotcha, my lady!" said the cop.

Manhattan wriggled. The crowd cheered. And the cop beamed as if it had been his idea all along.

"There y'are, sonny," he said, handing down the struggling Manhattan. "Who d'you say it belongs to?"

"Mr. Cape," said Peter, putting her into the basket and swinging down the lid. "Thank you ever so much."

"Oh," grunted the policeman. "Thought he said something about a member of the city council . . . Anyway," he straightened up, smiling, "don't go losing her again. I might not be on duty next time."

Peter and Benjie thanked him again.

Then, very quickly, they made their way through the crowd, which was itself beginning to disperse.

"We'll be lucky if news of this doesn't get back to the apartment," muttered Peter, suddenly feeling anxious again. "Come on! At least we can get her settled in before five."

9

Hugh Brodie—Detective

Peter was right about the news getting back to the apartment. They would have been lucky indeed if it hadn't. In fact it was a wonder it didn't beat them to it.

For New York apartment building doormen have ears that can pick up news items anywhere within a ten-block radius. They have eyes that can peer around every corner and into every recess inside a similar area, without their feet ever leaving the front doorstep. Are there a hundred people living in a particular doorman's building? Then there are two hundred eyes and two hundred ears working for him there. Are there ten, fifteen, twenty of those people taking an afternoon stroll in the vicinity? Just double whatever the number happens to be, and you'll have a pretty accurate tally of the eyes or ears working for that doorman—storing up items of information to be delivered to him as he opens the door and says, "Had a nice walk?"

Occasionally, of course, some of these eyes and ears will go blind and deaf on a doorman. It happened with Chico that afternoon as he smiled down at Peter and Benjie.

"Had a nice walk, you guys?"

"Oh . . . yes . . . fine, fine!" said Peter, keeping the basket on the side away from Chico.

"Just fine," said Benjie, who always believed in leaving the talking to Peter in such circumstances.

"Been shopping?" asked Chico, bending sideways to get a better look at the basket.

"Yes—I mean no," said Peter. He gave the elevator button another push. "Picnic," he said. "Sort of."

"Ah . . . over in the park, huh?" said Chico. "Nice over there. You got parks like that in London?"

"Plenty," mumbled Peter, glancing up at the flickering floor numbers over the elevator door and wishing it would hurry.

Manhattan stirred in the basket. Peter swung it casually behind him, then held it there.

"You sure weren't gonna starve, were you?" said Chico.

"Pardon?"

"Big hamper like that. Whatcha take in there?"

"Oh . . . food," said Peter, thankful to hear the sound of the elevator.

"Just food," said Benjie.

The elevator door slid open. Manhattan stirred again, more noisily this time, as a woman with a small terrier dog stepped out.

"Yurrrgh!" went the dog, suddenly straining at its leash and rearing in the air in front of the basket.

"Yow!" came the mournful reply from the basket.

Then quickly the boys went inside and pressed the button for their floor.

"Whew!" gasped Benjie, bending to the basket. "That was a close one!"

"Leave it!" snapped Peter. "We're on TV remember!"

But it was all wasted. Whether Chico had noticed the dog's reaction and the noise from the basket or not (and probably he'd been too busy beating the

lady to the door) there were other eyes and ears
—and tongues—at work that afternoon. And by the
time Mr. and Mrs. Clarke arrived back, shortly after
five, Chico was in full possession of the facts. Must
have been, thought Peter in a flash, as his father came
storming into the apartment like a police captain in
charge of a raid.

"Right!" thundered the man, slamming a fist down
on the table and sending Manhattan scooting under
the sofa. "I want a word with you, all of you: Adam!
Benjamin!—and *you!*"

He had more than one word with them that evening. And, besides the table, he thumped practically
every available surface, including the kitchen counter,
the desk, the sideboard, and a valuable antique tall-
boy. "I've never seen him so mad," confessed Adam,
afterward. "Just like a bongo player, all that thumping!"

At one point, hoping to deflect his father's wrath
away from himself, Benjie produced his Complaints
Book, in which he'd made a few entries about Peter
since their return with the cat, such was the prickli-
ness that developed in the waiting period. But:

"Don't come to me with piffling tales, boy!" roared
his father, sending the notebook flying in a fluttering
arc all across the room. "Look to your *own* behavior
—that's all I ask."

At another point it was Adam who came under
fire. During Peter's stumbling confession, he'd laughed
at the bit about the cat jumping on the policeman's
back.

"*You* needn't sit sniggering, lad!" cried Mr. Clarke, giving his right mustache a violent tug that brought his head around fullface to his eldest son. "If you'd been keeping a livelier eye on them, it wouldn't have happened. In future you *will!* Right?"

Adam gave a cross between a nod and a shrug.

"All rightee," he drawled, the way he'd heard a bus driver say it that afternoon. "Orrl ridee . . ."

"And speak English! You sound like a Chinese telling his family to get in the car."

"O.K.," said Adam, lowering his eyes.

"That's better!" growled Mr. Clarke. "Now, where were we? . . ."

Where they were was just coming up to the lecture he'd reserved for Peter, the major culprit. And at this point he stopped thumping the table and he lowered his voice. Peter himself wished that his father hadn't—that he'd gone on banging and storming. But it was always the same when he was the cause of the trouble. It was always a grave, almost sad speech which began with how surprised his father was, then worked its way through the bit about knowing it wasn't willfulness, and on to the bit about thoughtlessness sometimes being worse than willfulness, and ended with his father's voice becoming even gentler and asking if he'd promise.

"Promise," mumbled Peter, his face all hot.

"That's all right then," said Mr. Clarke. "The cat is not to leave this flat under any circumstances . . . And now the matter is closed. All's well that ends well. So dry those eyes, lad. . . ."

This was the standard ending. It used to infuriate Peter.

"I wouldn't mind!" he said to Benjie afterward, when they were on their own. "But I *never* cry till he says that, says dry those eyes, lad. . . . And what's the point getting me to promise a thing like that? As if I *would* take the cat out again after what happened."

"I wonder who told him?" said Benjie, whose own thoughts always turned to vengeance on such occasions.

"Chico, of course," sniffed Peter.

"Yes, but who told Chico?"

"Don't know," grunted Peter. "Someone from these apartments, I suppose. Someone who happened to be in the park. Someone—"

He stopped. His eyes went wide.

"*I* know! I bet *I* know who it was! That kid. The one who said he'd climb the tree if he hadn't his new pants on. . . ."

"The rat!" said Benjie, not sure who Peter meant, but happy to have someone to wreak his revenge on. "Let's get him!"

Peter wasn't anywhere near as belligerent as his brother. But he had very strong views about being gotten into trouble.

"I'll let him know what I think of him, if that's what you mean. And right now. He said he lived in 5E, didn't he?"

Peter pressed the bell button on the door of Apartment 5E.

"What're you going to say?" whispered Benjie.

"I'm going to give him a piece of my mind," said Peter.

"What if he doesn't like it?" asked Benjie.

"Too bad!" grunted Peter.

He gave the bell another push.

"Maybe there's no one in," suggested Benjie.

"I've heard someone moving about, just behind the door. Probably him."

"Bet he's watching us through the spy-hole," said Benjie. He stuck his tongue out at it—then dodged back behind Peter as the door opened.

The boy who'd spoken to Peter in the park was standing there, blinking at them through his glasses.

"Hi!" he said. "It's only those English kids."

He addressed the first remark to Peter and Benjie; the second, with a jerk of his head, to a girl standing behind him.

She came forward at that, and stared at them. Benjie too was feeling bolder by now and had come out from behind Peter.

"He was sticking his tongue out at the door, Hugh," said the girl, pointing at Benjie.

She was about ten years old, with brown frizzy hair and a lot of freckles. Her face had the round, slightly solemn look of the boy she'd addressed as Hugh. Peter guessed they were brother and sister.

"It's an old English custom," said Hugh. "There's a certain kind of Englishman can't resist sticking his tongue out at a closed door."

He winked at Peter and Peter was just about to wink and grin back when he remembered his mission.

"I want to see you," he said.

"Well I ain't invisible," said Hugh. "Far from it," he added, patting his shirt front and this time winking at Benjie.

Benjie laughed and winked back. Peter frowned at his brother. That was always the trouble with Benjie. Spitting blood and swearing vengeance one minute; swapping winks and vowing eternal friendship the next.

"I've come to see you about the cat," said Peter, sternly.

"Oh, *that!*" said Hugh. "Sorry I couldn't be of any assistance. But you did get her back in the end, didn't you?"

Peter and Benjie looked at each other and exchanged nods. Hugh laughed and nudged his sister.

"See that?" he said. "The way they looked then? Just like Friday and Gannon."

The girl smiled for the first time.

"Do it again," she said.

"Who's Friday and Gannon?" asked Peter.

"Couple of detectives on television. . . . Look, don't let's stand here, fellers. Come on in."

Peter caught himself exchanging another nod with Benjie and this time the girl laughed out loud.

Peter felt his face go red. This wasn't working out at all as he'd planned it. He was about to refuse when he realized that he was the only one left in the corridor. The others were inside, including Benjie.

He followed them into an apartment that was laid out exactly like Mr. Cape's: long living room in front, ending in French windows and a balcony overlooking the river; kitchen to the left; bathroom and other rooms to the right. It wasn't as elegantly furnished as Mr. Cape's though. Peter had an impression of lots of plants in pots, and odd shoes and other articles strewn about. The table hadn't been cleared after the evening meal, either—apart from one corner, where the dirty plates and cups had been pushed aside to make room for the first wriggling beginnings of a jig-saw picture. The girl had gone to sit in front of this. Her brother was at the French windows.

"Our folks are at a movie show," he said. "They left Sarah here in charge of the clearing up and me in charge of her. My name's Hugh, as you've probably guessed. His is Peter, Sarah, and the one with the tongue is Benjie, short for Benjamin."

"Hi!" said Sarah, glancing up briefly from her puzzle. "Hi . . ."

"How—how did you know?" asked Peter. "Our names, I mean . . ."

"Oh, he gets to know everything around here," said Sarah, this time without looking up. "Sometimes before it's even happened."

Peter remembered the cat again.

"Yes," he said. "And he sees to it that everyone else gets to know too!"

"Yeah!" growled Benjie. "You're the one with the tongue!"

Hugh blinked at them.

"What is this?" he said. "You seem like you're sore at something. Do you—?" He broke off at the sound of a whistling outside. "Excuse me a minute," he said. "I was just in the middle of something when you came. Why don't you come out here with me?"

Peter and Benjie followed him on to a balcony pretty much like their own, except that it was a lot nearer to the street and its noises.

But Hugh was looking up—at the line of balconies jutting out on his left. Four floors farther up, a dark brown face was peering over the railings.

"Thought you'd gone to bed, man!" bawled the owner of the face, a boy of about thirteen or fourteen, whom Peter had never seen before.

Hugh gave a cluck of annoyance.

"How d'you like that?" he said to Peter and Benjie. "I'm trying to teach him Silent Communications and he hollers for all the block to hear!"

He raised his hands and waved them, once inward, once out.

"That means, 'Please use Silent Communications,'" Hugh explained.

"Argh, forget it!" bawled the boy above, with a throwaway wave of the arm. Then he disappeared.

Hugh sighed.

"See that?" he murmured. "Waste of words. That wave *means* 'Forget it!' . . . But he's only just beginning. It gets them like that at first."

"What is it—a code?" asked Peter.

"Can we do it?" asked Benjie.

"Yes. And sure," said Hugh, answering them both.

"What's the idea of it?" asked Peter. "What's its use? I mean why *shouldn't* you just shout?"

Hugh gave another faint sigh and shook his head slightly.

"You're a bit dumb, ain't you, for an Englishman? The reason we don't just shout is because some of the kids are a lot farther up than Carl there—the one we saw just now. And with a police bull horn you'd never get your message across, the noise there is down below. And besides—you might as well say why not use the telephone. We all have phones."

"Well, why don't you?" asked Benjie.

"Because there are some messages you might not want your folks to hear."

Peter was nodding. "So you made up this sign language?"

"Silent Communications," said Hugh. "Yeah. It's still in its early stages, you know. Still being added to, developed. But some of the kids are getting real good at it."

"How d'you know when to start—to—er—silently communicate?" asked Peter, suddenly anxious to prove beyond all doubt that Englishmen are indeed most certainly *not* dumb. "I mean if you can't yell or use the phone?"

Hugh was frowning.

"It's one of the problems we haven't figured out yet," he said. "Sometimes it's just a prearranged time. Sometimes you do use the phone—but only to say 'See you out on the balcony.' Sometimes—if it's near enough—you whistle. Though that's not satisfactory . . ."

"Anyway, show us some of the signs," said Benjie.

"All rightee," said Hugh, raising his fist in the air and slowly bringing it down to the top of his head. "That means I can't make it, they're pinning me down, they won't let me go out."

He shot out an arm horizontally—once, twice, three times.

"That's three—that's the way you make numbers." He shot out an arm again, then left it there, slowly chopping down on it at the elbow with his other hand. "That's half. So three followed by that would mean three and a half or three-thirty. Probably three-thirty . . . Where's your balcony? You're in 12D, aren't you?"

He leaned out, peering up to his left and counting. Benjie beat him to it.

"There! Where that woman's leaning over, only it isn't a woman it's my brother Adam who's got long hair."

"I see it," said Hugh. "Well that should be O.K. There's a clear view here to there. Sometimes," he continued, his face clouding a little, "sometimes it gets awful complicated. When you're directly in line, up and down, and a dozen floors away. Then it's impossible without doing it through an intermediary— you know: a third person, on a balcony you *can* see . . ."

"I know, I know," said Peter, still smarting at being considered even a trifle dumb. "But—"

"And look—there's Manhattan!" cried Benjie. "Manhattan's out there with Adam!"

Sure enough, they could just make out the small round head that was poking through the railings at the side.

"I wish Adam would look," said Benjie. "I'd send him a message." He turned to Hugh. "How d'you say 'Get lost!' in Silent Combinations?"

"Silent *Communications*," said Peter, not wanting the accusation of dumbness to be leveled even at his —admittedly dumb—younger brother.

"The same as 'Forget it!'—the one Carl was doing up there." Hugh gave the throwaway wave. "That means all those things: 'Forget it!', 'Get lost!', 'Later, baby!'"

"Right," murmured Benjie, silently communicating this message to Adam. "Get lost!"

But Adam still wasn't looking, wasn't even aware of them. Only Manhattan was in a position to receive that message. . . .

Once again, Peter remembered what he'd come for.

"About that cat, Hugh," he said. "You know: in the park this afternoon."

"Oh, yeah, that . . . As I was saying, I'm sorry I wasn't able to help there. I was—"

"I'm not talking about that. We managed all right. We're not dumb, you know. . . . But what I *am* talking about is you getting us into trouble—telling Chico or—"

"Aw, now look here, feller! What makes you think *I* told Chico?"

"You were there, in the park. You saw what happened."

Hugh shook his head and led the way back into the apartment.

"You English sure *can* be dumb! At times . . ." He went to the table and picked up a plate. "Have a cookie. . . ."

Peter shook his head and continued to stare at Hugh accusingly. Benjie took two of the cookies. Sarah, without looking up from the puzzle, said: "Have some milk with them, won't you?"

Hugh fetched some glasses and began pouring milk from a pitcher. As he did so, he was saying:

"There were more people than me over there. Golly! These apartments are *full* of folks who go over into the park nice afternoons. I saw three, four, five, *six* of them this afternoon, around the time I saw you!"

"If they're there, Hughie'll see them!" murmured Sarah, in a tone that was part resignation and part admiration, stuck together with sarcasm.

"Anyway," said Hugh, "what trouble?"

"Our father and mother," said Peter. "Chico told them as soon as they got back."

Hugh was pushing the glasses of milk across to the brothers. He looked up sharply.

"And what time was that?"

"Just after five."

Hugh laughed and picked up his own glass.

"That proves it then! I didn't get back here until just after six!"

"Then *he* got into trouble," said Sarah, turning one of the jigsaw pieces this way and that. "On account of coming home late on movie night."

"I'll bet you it was Miss Salinsky," said Hugh. "13B. She was there in the park. She was in the crowd under the tree. And she's *always* back by four."

Peter no longer felt that it had been Hugh who had betrayed them. But he was beginning to get suspicious about the other's detailed knowledge of the apartment building and its inhabitants.

"How d'you know? Four o'clock every day? How d'you know?"

"Four o'clock every *week*day," Hugh said. "I know because she's crazy about "Secret Storm." . . . That's a television serial. Four o'clock every weekday. And she never misses an installment. Writes letters to the studio."

"You really do know a lot about the people here," murmured Peter.

"I tell you," said Sarah.

"I guess it comes naturally," said Hugh. "I practice a lot, too."

"He's going to be a detective when he leaves college," said Sarah.

"So am I!" cried Benjie.

"Well . . . not really a detective," said Hugh. "A kind of master detective—a lawyer really—a D.A. You know what that—?"

"District Attorney, yes," said Peter. "I've seen them on television."

"You have to know a lot about detective work for that," said Hugh. "You can't start practicing early enough."

"He collects fingerprints," said Sarah.

Hugh blushed slightly.

"Well, just friends' prints really . . ."

"And he plays memory games with me."

"They *are* useful," said Hugh, seriously.

"What about disguises?" asked Benjie.

"Kid stuff," said Hugh.

"He can remember all kinds of name plates, registration numbers," said Sarah.

"Useful," grunted Hugh. "Very useful."

"And telephone numbers."

"Sometimes Dad asks *me*, saves him looking in the directory."

"What's ours then?" asked Peter. "What's Mr. Cape's?"

"Riverside 2-9970," said Hugh, without a pause.

"Gosh!" said Benjie.

"I'll check," said Peter, who hadn't memorized it himself.

"You'll see," said Sarah.

"He's right!" said Peter, looking up from the directory. He laughed. "Hugh," he said, "if we ever need a detective we'll send for you!"

"Aw, well now . . ." began Hugh.

"You do that," said Sarah, solemnly.

"We will!" said Benjie.

"We most certainly will!" said Peter, still laughing.

That was on a Tuesday. Only two days later—by the Thursday of that same week—they had reason to remember those words. And this time there was no laughing.

For, on the Thursday afternoon, Peter and Benjie really did need a detective. On the Thursday afternoon, Manhattan disappeared, completely, and without warning. It was almost as if the cat had, after all, intercepted that "Get lost!" message Benjie had intended for Adam—intercepted it and acted upon it.

10

Manhattan Is Missing

What had happened?

Who was to blame?

Those were the questions that everyone was to keep on asking for a long time. And at first the only firm answer that was given to either of them came from Peter, Benjamin, and Adam. Each had vague theories and misgivings about the other two boys, of course; but each was absolutely positive that he himself wasn't to blame.

Again and again, Peter went over the incidents that had occurred in the two intervening days: between the afternoon that they had, admittedly, nearly lost the cat, to the afternoon that Manhattan disappeared.

"I mean, after what had happened on Tuesday I was extra careful. It stands to sense!"

This he kept saying to anyone prepared to listen to him—and when there was no one else to tell it to, he'd say it to himself. In the bathtub, for example, as he lay gazing at Manhattan's unused tray until the water around him grew cool. Or out on the balcony, as he tried to calculate for the hundredth time where the cat might have jumped from there—and lived. Or at night, in bed, with the slatted bluey-green light across his bed, across the spot where Manhattan herself had lain for the first three nights. Sometimes, as he dozed off, he fancied he could feel her softly kneading the clothes over his chest, preparing a place to settle on. Sometimes he had the feeling that she was asleep, lying across his knees, a contented prisoner behind those bars of shadow. But when he eased himself up there was no cat, not even a flattened warmer patch on the covers. Then, fully awake again, he would remind himself once more how careful he had been.

In any case, it wasn't as if he'd wanted to take the cat out again, even into the corridors, after the trip to the park. Hadn't there been better things to do? Hadn't both he and Benjie made some new friends? Hadn't they spent those two days mainly with Hugh and Sarah—exploring Riverside Park, which the English boys were astonished to find stretched for miles and miles; visiting the even bigger Central Park farther inland; helping Sarah with the jigsaw puzzle; practicing Silent Communications with Hugh; getting to know Carl and some of the other children in the block; going to the shops on Broadway? Hadn't their time been fully taken up learning new games, new words, new kinds of food?

Not that he'd been *neglecting* Manhattan—Peter would remind himself at this point, feeling a little guilty. Every morning, he'd seen to her tray and her food and taken her on to the balcony for her grooming. And, after meals, or last thing at night, or whenever they were in the apartment, both he and Benjie had spent some time playing with the cat, trailing string for her, or picking up the pencils and combs and other light objects she used to love to flick off the desk and tables and sideboard—picking these things up and setting them up for her again. Once they had even invited Hugh and Sarah in to play the fly-catching game with her.

In spite of his anxiety, Peter would smile when he thought of this. Hugh had told them about it. Apparently, Mr. Cape's cleaning lady had told Hugh's mother about it one day, about how it was a favorite game that her own son used to play with Manhattan.

"That cat can't bear flies to come into the apartment," Hugh had explained. "She'll spend hours chasing just one."

"I've seen her," Peter said.

"So have I," said Benjie.

"Well then—Tony, the cleaning lady's kid, used to help Manhattan, pick her up, help her get those up near the ceiling, *train* her at them, like a gun. Why don't we do that? Why don't we make a contest of it . . . while Adam's out of the way? Why don't we open the windows and the balcony door, let some flies in, then take it in turns, ten minutes each? See how many we can help her to catch. . . ."

And so they had. The score: Hugh 2, Peter 1, Benjie 0, Sarah −1. (A penalty point for allowing Manhattan to scratch the wallpaper.)

The more Peter had seen of Hugh, the more he'd liked the American boy. For one thing, he was full of bright ideas—like the fly hunt, the Silent Communications system, his collection of fingerprints, and his memory-training games. But better even than that was the fact that between Hugh's ideas and his actual performances, there was often a gap. His success at the fly hunt had been real enough, if a bit of a fluke; but his Silent Communications system was far from perfect, his fingerprint collection in such a muddle that he wasn't sure whether one set belonged to his mother or to Chico, and his memory for numbers not always reliable—as when he'd tried to telephone a delicatessen store by dialing his father's Social Security number. . . .

That was not long after they'd decided Manhattan was really missing. "We'll ask the delicatessen store to post a notice," he'd said. "They're always posting descriptions of lost pets."

A typical Hugh Brodie idea—prompt, bright—followed by a typical bit of Hugh Brodie bungling, over the telephone number. . . .

Hugh and Sarah had been with them when the cat's disappearance was first noted. They had been across in the park, where Hugh had been teaching the English boys the rudiments of baseball and—what with the arguments and counterarguments, the cries of encouragement and the shouts of disgust—they'd worked up a thirst.

"We've got lots of orange juice," said Peter. "Let's go up to our apartment. Adam won't be back yet."

"And it's all the same if he is," said Benjie, whose stay in New York was making him more aggressive than ever. "It's not *his* juice. Come on, youse guys!"

He was still bragging about what he'd say (and, if necessary, do) to Adam, when Peter let them in with the key that he'd collected from the doorman.

"Oh, shut up, Benjie!" said Peter. He grinned at Hugh. "He knows he's safe," he explained. "With the key being down with the doorman. He knows perfectly well that that means Adam *is* still out."

"I hadn't even thought," said Benjie. "*I'm* not scared of Adam!"

"Where's Manhattan?" asked Sarah, pausing at the

open door. "Doesn't she come to meet you? Flicker does, the cat in the next apartment to us."

"Not always," said Peter. "She's probably out on the balcony. Or maybe asleep in one of the other rooms. Come on in, anyway."

Hugh and Sarah went to the balcony. Peter and Benjie got the orange juice, the glasses, and a pitcher of water.

"Ladies first," said Sarah.

"Where are they?" said Benjie, looking up, down, around.

"Ladies should do all the pouring and passing around," said Hugh. "Give Peter a hand, sister dear."

"I don't mind," said Sarah. "What about Manhattan? Shall we give her some milk? Where is she?"

"She must be in one of the other rooms," said Peter. "No . . . Here . . . It's all right . . . Let me pour. You're drowning it."

So they sat or leaned on the balcony, quenching their thirsts, and looking out at the river, where a heavy, hot afternoon haze was slowly building up from the north, obscuring the George Washington Bridge.

"It's hotting up out here," said Benjie. "Let's go in. Let's find Manhattan and have a fly hunt. Me first."

"Second!" cried Sarah.

"Kids!" sighed Hugh, shaking his head. "I don't mind though. Peter?"

"Sure!" said Peter. "I'll go and get her."

But she was not to be found in the boys' bedroom. Nor was she to be found in their parents' bedroom.

"That's funny," said Peter.

"She'll be hiding," said Benjie. "Come on, Manhattan! Flies! Chase 'em!"

From briefly glancing around the rooms, looking in the obvious places, they began to search more thoroughly.

"Do you mind?" asked Hugh, pausing at a clothes-closet door.

"Go ahead, go ahead," murmured Peter, on his knees, peering under Adam's bed. "Anywhere . . ."

Already he was beginning to feel the tingle of panic running through his limbs. . . .

But Manhattan was nowhere in the apartment.

"O.K.," said Hugh. "So let's see if she slipped out to do a little visiting."

"Slipped out?" said Peter. "How? When? She was in when we left."

"And she didn't slip out when we got back," said Benjie.

"You were too busy yacking to notice," said Peter.

"*I* wasn't, though," said Sarah, quietly. "I was looking for her. I was expecting her. Remember?"

"Are you *sure* she was in when you left?" asked Hugh.

"Well—yes . . ." murmured Peter, trying to visualize their departure.

"I *think* so . . ." said Benjie.

"I—yes—I'm *sure*," said Peter. "I remember wondering whether to close the balcony door to keep the hot air from getting in. Then I saw Manhattan was out there—"

"What doing?" said Hugh suddenly, making Sarah jump.

"Oh, just poking her head through the railings as usual. Anyway, I left the door open for her—the balcony door."

"And she sure couldn't go any farther than here," said Hugh, stepping out and peering over the railings.

"Maybe she jumped," said Benjie.

Peter went prickly at the backs of his legs.

"Ner . . ." said Hugh, peering over. "If she had we'd have heard about it. The sidewalk's always busy down there. And it's a long drop."

"To the next balcony, I mean," said Benjie.

Hugh had another look down. Peter joined him.

"It's possible, I suppose," said Hugh.

"If she managed to curve inwards in mid-air, between here and there," said Peter.

"Oh, golly!" groaned Sarah.

"She's never been known to try it," said Hugh. "In all the years she's been here . . . But I guess there's always a first time."

"That's what I say," said Benjie.

"We'll go down to 11D and ask," said Hugh.

The elderly gentleman in 11D looked quite startled when he opened the door to find four such grave-faced children standing there. He looked even more startled when one of them—a plump boy with glasses —addressed him by his name and then rapped out:

"We're investigating a missing animal, sir—cat, female, Siamese—maybe you can help us."

But the gentleman in 11D was unable to help them in their investigations, beyond supplying them with the negative information that no cat had landed on *his* balcony that afternoon, because he'd been sitting out there himself from about 2:30 on.

"And none's gone flying past, sir?" Peter made himself ask.

"Flying past? A flying cat?" The man stared down at Peter. "You're English, aren't you?"

It wasn't so much a question as an answer—a suggestion that only the English would be crazy enough to believe in the existence of flying cats—here in the center of civilization of all places.

"I drink water with my bourbon," he added, gently closing the door in their faces.

"What's that got to do with it?" asked Sarah.

"What's bourbon?" asked Benjie.

But Peter and Hugh were already on their way to the elevator.

Back on the twelfth floor, they gave the rest of it a thorough check. First they investigated the laundry room, even removing the lids of the washer and drier, in case Manhattan had climbed up to investigate, found a lid partly open, squeezed through, and caused the lid to fall back properly.

No luck.

Then they investigated the small room where the garbage chute was, shuddering at the thought of Manhattan's managing somehow to claw open the bulky iron door.

"Too heavy," said Hugh, opening it himself and swiveling back the part with the built-up sides, on which the garbage was placed before being shot into the hole that ran down from floor to floor, past other chutes and into a furnace.

A faint whiff of sooty smoke made Peter shudder again.

"I suppose—could it have been left partly open?"

"Impossible!" said Hugh, letting go. The door swung smoothly, swiftly back with a dull clang. "Designed never to stick. And checked by the engineer every day—just in case."

"Because of cats falling through?" asked Benjie.

"Because of fumes drifting back," said Hugh. "C'm on. We'll ask the folks on this floor if they've seen her."

But there was no luck there either—beyond the fact that someone happened to be home in each of the other nine apartments on that floor. In tones varying from deep sympathy through curiosity to brisk annoyance at having to answer the door for such a query, the answer was the same. No Manhattan.

"Well, I guess we'd better ask Chico now," said Hugh.

"Oh not *him!*" cried Benjie, remembering Tuesday.

"We'll have to," said Peter. "It doesn't matter if he does tell Mum and Dad. They'll get to know anyway, if we don't find her."

"Think of all the people we've already asked," said Sarah, following the two older boys.

"Wait for me then," said Benjie.

Chico's eyes widened as they all came toward him.

"What's this?" he asked, smiling. "Ready for the command performance?"

Even then Peter's spirits sank. Obviously the door-man had heard nothing about the cat yet. No one had called down to tell him there was a stray on their corridor. Obviously.

Chico groaned as they explained what had happened.

"Oh *no!*" he groaned. "Oh, brother!"

"So you've had no reports?"

"Oh, brother!" Without replying, Chico went over to his intercom set and began pressing buttons. "Where is the guy?" he kept muttering, as he pressed, listened, pressed again.

"What's he doing?" whispered Peter.

"Trying to get hold of somebody," said Hugh. "Probably Alfredo—the engineer. He's always moving around the building—yes."

"Ah, Alfredo, my brother. Cómo estás panín? . . . Listen . . ."

Half in English, half in another language, he began questioning the engineer. The children listened, frowning at the bits they couldn't understand, straining their ears to catch every expression and tone in the engineer's voice as it came spluttering and echoing through the grille.

"What are they talking?" whispered Benjie.

"Spanish," said Hugh. "Puerto Ricans . . . Be quiet. . . ."

Chico looked worried when he finally turned back to them.

"Alfredo's heard nothing . . . yet. When you find out?"

They told him everything they knew.

He nodded rapidly, point by point.

"O.K.," he said, when they'd finished and were looking up at him hopefully, all silent and still, as if they expected him suddenly to laugh and produce Manhattan from under his coat. "O.K., O.K., I'll ask around. I'll keep asking. Someone must know something."

But he was still looking very worried as he watched them go.

On the way back up, Hugh started going over it all again.

"You *sure* you left her in the apartment?"

"On the balcony, yes."

"With access to the apartment?"

"Yes."

"And you closed the apartment door properly when you left?"

"Yes."

"Sure?"

"Positive . . . I was in charge of the key, remember. Adam had gone out. So I was extra careful."

As they got out of the elevator, Hugh smacked his hands together.

"Hey!" he said. "Adam! You sure he didn't come back while you were out? Maybe he came back, found the cat sick or something, and took her to the veterinarian's!"

Peter opened the apartment door and went straight to Manhattan's cupboard. Her carrying basket was still there. Empty.

"I doubt it," he said. "Anyway, the key was still with Chico when we got back."

"Yeah, well . . . Adam could have come back for something and gone out again—and he'd have left the key with Chico just the same. Maybe *he* was careless and let the cat slip out. I'll check."

But Chico's voice was sadly firm as it rattled out of the loudspeaker grille.

"Nobody—but nobody—took that key between Peter leaving it and collecting it again."

"Where d'you keep it?" asked Hugh.

Chico's voice had an angry rasp as he replied.

"What you trying to say, baby? That I go to sleep on the job, huh? That I let people snick up and borrow the keys left with me?"

"No, no . . ."

"I keep him in my pocket, baby. I told you—nobody—but no *body*—"

"O.K.K.K.K. *Kay!*" protested Hugh, switching off.

It wasn't really rudeness that caused him to cut Chico off so abruptly. In matters of this sort, as Peter was beginning to learn, Hugh's mind worked fast—

probing in several different directions at once. Even as he'd been talking to the doorman he'd had another hunch, another little stab of response to one of the probes.

"Look," he said, turning to the others and then beginning to glance around the room. "Maybe there *was* someone in here while you were out. Not Adam. Maybe not anyone we know. But someone who didn't need the key—who could get in without it—with a skeleton key maybe or some kind of a tool."

"A thief?"

Hugh nodded.

"We get cases sometimes. One last month. Usually in the afternoons, too. This one might have slipped in while you were out."

He spoke as if he was now sure that that was what had happened. But Peter was doubtful. As he and Benjie went from room to room, checking, his doubt increased. No locked drawers had been forced. No closets had been rifled. There were no clothes strewn about, except in the boys' room—and that was only the normal strewing of pajamas and dirty shirts and so on that Mrs. Clarke was always complaining about. Most significant of all, none of the obvious valuables was missing—none of the ornaments or paintings that Mr. Cape had appeared to be so anxious about.

Only the cat.

"But who'd go to all that trouble to steal a cat?" asked Peter.

Hugh nodded. His mind was still probing, probing . . .

"Maybe a thief did get in. Maybe he was disturbed. Maybe he left before he'd time to take anything. And maybe the cat just slipped out, as we were saying at first. Or—wait—could either your father or your mother have come back for something?"

"Chico would have said . . ."

"Or—listen—how many keys are there?"

"We have two. One they leave with us . . . one they take with them."

"And Mr. Cape'll have one, that's three . . ." Hugh murmured. "I wonder . . ."

"What? If Mr. Cape's come back and—"

"Oh be quiet, Benjie! Go on, Hugh. What were you wondering?"

Mention of their father and mother had made Peter look at his watch. And it was nearly five o'clock.

"Mrs. Walsh," said Hugh.

"Oh yes!" cried Sarah, quite loud for her.

"Mrs. Walsh might have a key," Hugh continued. "She probably does."

"Who's she?" asked Benjie.

"Cleaning lady," said Peter. "But she comes Mondays, Hugh. That's what Mr. Cape told us."

"Yes, but she cleans some of the other apartments here. Maybe she ran out of soap or something. Came in here where she knew there was some. Or came to check on something. Came in, anyway. And let the cat slip out."

Before any of the others could comment, he was back on the intercom, questioning Chico.

Yes. Mrs. Walsh had been in the building. Someplace on the sixth floor. No. She'd left at about four. And no. She'd said nothing about the Cape apartment.

"I'll call her myself, just to check," said Hugh, after he'd switched off. "I know her number. She cleans for us."

Actually he'd forgotten—as he realized himself after first getting a supermarket and then one of his mother's old schoolfriends in Jersey City. But Mrs. Walsh was in the book and he was soon connected.

"Hello, who's this? Tony? Your mother there, Tony? . . . Hugh Brodie . . . Riverdrive View . . . Yeah . . . Tell her it's urgent. . . ." Hugh turned from the phone. "Her kid. Tony. She's in. She . . . Hi, Mrs. Walsh! Sorry to bother you. But were you in the Cape apartment at all this afternoon? . . . You sure? . . . Er—well—we're just having a kind of a game, Mrs. Walsh, kind of guessing game, memory game, sort of . . . Er . . ."

The others could hear the faint rattle of a rapid, angry voice. They watched Hugh's ears get redder and redder.

"I'm sorry, Mrs. Walsh . . . Honest . . . I didn't know you were in the tub . . . Tony didn't . . . Yes, Mrs. Walsh."

Hugh was shaking his head as he put down the telephone. His ears were red and he still looked glum, but he'd gotten the information he required.

"No," he said. "She didn't come near the apartment."

Peter sighed.

"We'd better make a note of some of these things," he said. "For the record. Dad'll be here soon. At least we can say we've been trying hard."

"I think I'll go over to the park for a bit," said Benjie, looking rather pale.

"Oh no you don't!" said Peter. "You're staying here with me."

"I think it's time *we* were going though," said Sarah.

"Yes," said Hugh. "Let me know how you make out, Peter. And keep thinking. This is getting really interesting."

"Interesting!" grunted Benjie. "It's all right for *them!* . . . What time is it now?"

11

Chico Breaks It Gently

Mr. and Mrs. Clarke were in very good spirits on
their way home in the bus that afternoon. They were
feeling the heat, and the bus had been crawling from
one traffic jam into another, but they could have been
purring along an empty road in an air-conditioned
limousine for all the difference these things made.
Mr. and Mrs. Clarke had had three very promising
interviews with publishers in various parts of the town
and an excellent lunch, and altogether it looked as if
their visit to New York was going to be even more
successful than they'd hoped.

"If we go on at this rate the trip will have paid
for itself inside two weeks," said Mr. Clarke.

"They'll be giving us medals when we get back,"
said Mrs. Clarke. "For boosting the export trade."

Mr. Clarke laughed.

"Oh, well, hardly *that!*"

Nevertheless, he settled more comfortably in his
seat and half-closed his eyes, musing on the idea.
Buckingham Palace . . . the Queen . . . "Rise, Sir
Bruce Clarke! . . ." for services to his country in the
export field . . . initiative . . . took the whole family
at great expense . . . drive . . .

Even when Adam got on the bus, Mr. Clarke wasn't upset.

"What are you doing here, my boy?"

Adam had the look of someone who'd been hurrying. He also had the look of someone inwardly cursing his appalling luck. Of all the buses to get on, he seemed to be thinking, why did it have to be *this?*

"Just been doing a bit of shopping, Dad," he mumbled.

Mr. Clarke nodded contentedly.

"That's all right, my boy. Not to worry. We never asked you to stay indoors all the time. Simply to make sure when you did go out that Peter and Benjie were sensibly occupied and that the apartment was secure. And, of course, not to be gone too long."

Adam brightened up.

"Oh yes . . . sure . . . we have a system."

It did cross Mr. Clarke's mind that systems required planning and that planning, in some circumstances, could amount to conspiracy, and that Adam must be in the habit of going out often during the day. In fact, had Adam's parents' business not gone so well, the home-going workers on that Number 19 bus might have been treated to a display of Mr. Clarke's indignation going full blast. Instead, the father smiled happily under his untugged mustache and said:

"Your mother and I have had a very good day, in case you're too shy to ask. . . ."

"Oh—er—yes—did you? Great!" Adam brightened up

again. "D'you mind if I bring Julie round to the apartment one day? Maybe for lunch?"

"Well . . ." Mr. Clarke frowned very slightly. "We'll have to see."

"Perhaps on Saturday, dear," suggested Mrs. Clarke, always ready to steer her sons through the dangerous currents of their father's moods. "When we're all at home."

Adam failed to respond.

"She called this morning," he began. "And—"

"You mean she's been already?" demanded Mr. Clarke.

He had stiffened. His hand was straying to his mustache.

"Oh no, Dad!"

"But you said she'd called!"

"On the phone."

"Ah! Another Americanism!" Mr. Clarke relaxed again. He smiled, unaware of the curious looks this last remark had attracted from some of their traveling companions.

"You see where it gets you, my boy. Causes confusion. Utter confusion."

"I think, Bruce, you might find the boy's knowledge of the American language jolly helpful when you get back home and have all these books to illustrate."

Thus, gently, Mrs. Clarke steered her husband back into sunnier, smoother waters.

"Hm! . . . well . . . Maybe you're right."

The thought of all the business he was doing returned, and with it the glow.

"I wonder what sort of a day Peter and Benjamin have had?" he murmured, as he helped his wife off the bus.

"They were fine when I left," said Adam. "They were going to play with that kid Hugh and his sister over in the park."

"Good! Good!" said Mr. Clarke. "I'm glad they've found some friends. . . . So long as they didn't take the cat again."

"Oh, they know better than that, dear!" said Mrs. Clarke. "After what happened on Tuesday . . . Thank you, Chico."

They had reached the doors of the apartment building. Chico was holding one open for them.

"Good evening, sir, ma'am. Hi, Adam . . . Have the boys been in contact with you yet?"

"In *contact?*"

"Yeah . . . With the news . . ."

Peter and Benjie didn't get to know exactly what Chico told their father and mother this time. But before his parents had been back five minutes, Peter was deciding that the doorman must have broken the news very gently indeed.

Mrs. Clarke said nothing. She looked pale and sat down without even putting the kettle on to make some tea. She seemed to be watching her husband more attentively than usual, more anxiously. Adam too was looking very worried as he quietly slipped out of the living room and went into the bathroom, where at once he began running the shower.

As for Mr. Clarke, he didn't shout, didn't tug his mustache, didn't thump the table. Fumbling with his glasses, he just said quietly: "Well, what happened?"

And while Peter and Benjie explained, telling him about how they'd first discovered Manhattan was missing, and their inquiries and theories and further inquiries, Mr. Clarke nodded glumly. He didn't interrupt beyond murmuring an occasional, "Yes, go on." He didn't snort or roll his eyes or groan. But he did slump. As the younger boys' account was unfolded, their father slumped further and further in his chair. The flesh under his eyes and on his cheeks and at the sides of his chin seemed to sag—to lose its firm rosiness and become puckered, flabby, yellowish-gray. Even his mustaches seemed to droop—like wilting ferns.

Then Peter began to realize that it was not just the fact that Chico had broken the news gently that had made his father go so surprisingly quiet and still. When Mr. Clarke was irritated or annoyed by some small or medium-sized upset he thumped tables and roared and pulled his mustaches—yes. But when he slumped and was quiet and gloomily civil, he was more than annoyed. He was really distressed. Peter had seen him like this on very few occasions before —and they were all very serious ones. Like the time their mother had fallen off the kitchen steps and had had to go to the hospital with a broken leg. Or the time when Benjie had got lost one evening and didn't come back until after midnight—in a police car. Or the time when some drawings, the result of ten weeks' hard work, had got lost in the post and his father had had them all to do again. . . .

"You see," said Mr. Clarke, quietly, gently, sadly, when Peter and Benjie had told him all they knew, "this—this could make a big difference. A horribly big difference. This could make the whole trip a disaster —financially—where money's concerned—however well we do later. You see, there's a big deposit on this place, this flat, this apartment."

"Deposit?" whispered Benjie, looking around and up at the ceiling, as if he thought his father was talking about a cloud of poisonous gas.

"Money, dear," explained Mrs. Clarke. "An amount of money that you have to put down—give to the owner."

"Rent?" asked Benjie.

"No," said his father—far more patient than he was when things were going better. "A sum of money besides the rent—which you give to the owner in case things get damaged. Or lost. If things are all right when he returns—if they're undamaged, not lost —he gives you your deposit back. If not—well—you could lose the lot."

"How—how much deposit did you pay Mr. Cape?" asked Peter.

Mr. Clarke sighed.

"Fifteen hundred dollars, I'm afraid. . . . Over six hundred pounds . . ."

12

"Operation Catnet"

That evening, just as the Clarke family was coming
to the end of a very subdued meal, there was a ring
at the door.

Mrs. Clarke answered. It was Hugh.

"Are Peter and Benjie ready yet?" he asked.

"It's getting rather late," said Mrs. Clarke. "We've
been—er—delayed rather."

"I know. That's why I came up looking for them.
. . . Hi, Peter! Hi, Benjie!"

The face that peered around the side of Mrs. Clarke
was the only one present that wasn't gloomy. Hugh
wasn't smiling, but his eyes were gleaming in a business-like eager way.

Mr. Clarke frowned. With something like his usual
manner, he gave his mustache a slight tug.

"I'm afraid Peter and Benjamin will not be available
this evening," he said. "Between now and their bed-
time they'll be helping to search for the cat."

"That's what I was figuring, sir," said Hugh. "That's
why I want to get started. We have some planning to
do."

"Planning?"

"Yes, sir. Just searching around anyplace is no good.

You've got to have system. Plan the operation properly so you don't waste time. Operation Catnet."

Mr. Clarke gave the table a light rap. Adam cast a "Here we go!" look at the ceiling. Mrs. Clarke began chewing her lip. And Peter tried, with a shake of the head, to warn Hugh to be careful what he was saying.

"Operation Balderdash! This is no time for games, boy! This is serious!"

"I know, sir. There's fifteen hundred bucks at stake."

"Eh? How the blazes—?"

"Chico, sir. You must have told him and he told my father when he came in. Probably been telling everybody. But I shouldn't worry, sir. It helps if folks know just how serious it is. Makes them look harder."

Mr. Clarke was silent now, looking hard himself— at the visitor.

"What an extraordinary boy!" he murmured at last. "Well, don't stand there, son. Come and sit down. Glass of milk?"

"If you don't mind, sir, I'd rather we got on the ball —you know—got down to business."

He looked at Peter and Benjie.

"Ready?"

"Oh, yes, sure . . ."

Peter and Benjie stood up.

"Well—just a minute," said Mr. Clarke. "What are your proposals? Where do *we* fit in?" He waved a hand between himself, his wife, and Adam.

Hugh frowned.

"I wasn't expecting—I mean I was figuring on just

us kids doing the main searching. We're here most of the day, you see. And besides—it's no use if there are too many people in charge."

"You mean—?"

"Not that I'm stopping you from searching in your own way, sir—you and Mrs. Clarke—and Adam. It all helps. Only *my* search I want to do *my* way."

Now it was Peter's turn to object.

"How d'you mean, *your* search?" he asked.

"Yeah!" added Benjie.

"It's our cat," said Peter.

"Mr. Cape's cat," corrected Hugh.

"It's in our care," said Peter.

"And it's gonna be our fifteen hundred dollars!" said Benjie, causing his father to wince.

Hugh had been nodding.

"But it's *my* neighborhood. We know the place, sir," he said, appealing to Mr. Clarke. "We know the district, the people, the likely places, the best places to inquire. That's why I say I should be in charge."

Mr. Clarke looked at Peter and Benjie.

"What he says makes sense," he said fiercely. "Do as he tells you."

"Thank you, sir," said Hugh, giving Peter and Benjie the ghost of a smirk. "Maybe you'd better get them to promise aloud."

"Yes," said Mr. Clarke. "Let's hear it. Do you promise to do as he tells you?"

"Huh!" grunted Benjie.

"*What?*" roared his father.

"Yes . . ." whispered Benjie.

"Better!" said Mr. Clarke. He turned to Peter: "You?"

Peter sighed.

"All right then, I promise. But only in things connected with the search."

Mr. Clarke looked at Hugh.

"Suits me," said the boy. "And now, sir, before we go someplace to get on with our planning, do I have your permission to offer a reward?"

"A reward?"

"I was thinking of twenty dollars, sir. To begin with, anyway. Sharpens people's eyes. I was thinking —again with your permission—to call the delicatessen right away and get them to post a notice. And I've one or two more places in mind as well."

"What an extraordinary boy!" gasped Mr. Clarke again, looking at his wife. "How old are you, son?"

"Twelve. Coming up thirteen in October. That's O.K. then? Twenty dollars?"

Mr. Clarke was sitting up straighter than he had been all evening. His face was still pale, but a sparkle had returned to his eyes, and his mustache was looking more like its old bristly self.

"Of course," he said. "You have my permission, Lieutenant."

And what made the rest of the Clarke family look at one another in wonder was the fact that he'd pronounced the last word the American way: "Lootenant."

Peter and Benjie were still rather stiff with their friend for some time afterward. Being ordered about by their parents was one thing. Being ordered about by a person only a little older than themselves, *nominated by their parents,* was quite another thing.

Not that Hugh threw his weight about or took advantage of the position in any unnecessary way. He

was far too busy suggesting things and then planning
ways of carrying them out. He was genuinely interested in making as good a job of the search as
possible. And there was no denying the fact that most
of his ideas were good, or, if not good in themselves, bright and interesting enough to stimulate other
ideas.

So, after stopping their faces from relaxing whenever they felt a smile or a look of eager agreement
taking shape, and after snickering smugly when Hugh
made his mistake in dialing the delicatessen's number, they gradually got over their annoyance.

"Did you say something about other notices?" asked
Peter, when Hugh had finished telephoning.

"Yes," said Hugh. "Here."

The boys were sitting on Hugh's bed in the Brodie
apartment. Sarah was sitting on the floor. Hugh
handed Peter a sheet of paper on which he'd scrib-
bled some words. "Read it," he said. "See if I've left
anything out."

Peter was still not *quite* ready to forgive Hugh.
So, with Benjie breathing over his shoulder, he puckered his mouth, ready to criticize harshly, as he read:

LOST CAT

Chocolate-pointed Siamese. Answers to "Manhattan". Riverside Drive area around W. 81.
Phone RIverside 2-9970 or RIverside 2-8099.

REWARD: 20 DOLLARS

"It's what you've just read out over the phone,"
said Peter, struggling to find something wrong.

"Sure. What I mean is do you like the way it's set out? The LOST CAT bit in capitals at the top and the reward in capitals at the bottom. Hits 'em with the essential details right away."

"You missed out 'Street,'" said Benjie. "West 81st Street."

"We never bother with that in New York," said Hugh.

"Besides, it saves a word," said Sarah. "And when you type as slow as I do, every word counts."

"Have you got a typewriter then?" asked Benjie, looking at the girl with new respect.

"No, it's mine," said Hugh. "I'm letting her do it as a favor."

"Big deal!" said Sarah, sounding far more bored than she looked.

"I see you've given your phone number as well," said Peter, with a faint bitterness.

"Makes sense," said Hugh. "In case no one's in for one of them."

"'Answers to' isn't strictly correct," said Peter. "She doesn't take much notice of her name. Cats don't. If you *must* put it, simply say 'called.' 'Called Manhattan.' And we'd better add 'female.'"

"Fine! fine!" said Hugh, scribbling in the amendments. "I'm glad you mentioned these things." He added the word "street" as well, saying: "Might as well make it perfectly clear."

And, by the time he'd finished and had given the notice to Sarah with instructions to make six copies, the two English boys were feeling much better about the whole thing.

Hugh's next job was to question the boys closely about Manhattan's habits, taking notes as he did so.

"I've borrowed a couple of books about cats," he explained. "To read up about their habits in general. Now I want to know about hers in particular. About her food, what she likes and doesn't like, when she sleeps most, that sort of thing. . . ."

Peter and Benjie answered willingly enough and soon Hugh had two pages full of notes. But it did strike Peter that most of them were unnecessary and, after a while, he said so.

"What's the use of noting the name of her favorite brand of cat food when she's lost? Or the fact that she loves to be brushed and combed?"

"Plenty," said Hugh, sucking the end of his pencil and frowning thoughtfully at the list. "It's giving me ideas already about equipment."

"Equipment?"

"Yeah! Equipment for the search . . . We've got to be ready in case we find her someplace several blocks away. All right: *one cat basket.*" He jotted the item down on a separate sheet of paper. "Also we have to have something to signal her with, in case she's lying low someplace, under cover, out of sight." He patted one of the cat books. "I've already found out cats usually do this. And now—from what you just told me—I know the best things to attract her attention with." He began writing. "One plastic bowl containing two brushes and a comb . . ."

"What's that got to do with it?"

"You say she comes running every morning, just

at the sound of the brushes being rattled, or the comb clinking on the bowl. O.K., then. Maybe she'll come running when she hears us making these noises near her hide-out." He began writing again. "Same with the sound of a fork on a saucer. That should fetch her out if she's hungry. . . . And in case there's too much traffic noise or something, we'll take a dish of this food all ready, and leave it to her sense of smell. . . ."

So, item by item, Hugh built up his equipment list until it read:

Operation Catnet—Basic Equipment
1 Cat basket
1 Plastic bowl containing 2 brushes, 1 comb
1 fork
1 saucer
1 can food (ready opened)
1 flashlight
1 set of paper and string cat toys—assorted

"O.K.," said Hugh, handing the completed list to Peter. "Get 'em. And be right back. . . . Sarah," he called out, "have you finished typing those notices yet?"

Ten minutes later, armed with the Basic Equipment and a bundle of notices, they set off on their second tour of the premises.

First they went down to the lobby.

"Found her then?" asked Pepe, the night doorman, who had taken over from Chico.

He was staring at the basket, his fat, smooth face bent hopefully forward.

"No—we're just making another search," explained Hugh. "Mind if we post this on the bulletin board?"

Pepe glanced at the notice.

"Go ahead."

He watched them as they pinned it up, next to the notices about returned laundry and cleaning women and baby sitters and the date the Jazzmobile van would be in the area.

"Verrry pretty . . ." murmured Pepe. "You done that real nice."

"Thanks," said Sarah, glowing a little.

"You have some more there?" he asked, glancing down at the bundle in her hand.

"Sure," said Hugh. "We're gonna put 'em in strategic places."

"Like where?" asked Pepe.

Hugh shrugged.

"I haven't figured exactly where yet, but we'll know 'em when we come to them."

"Give me some," said Pepe. "How many you got? . . . This *all?*"

"We can do some more," said Peter. "Can't we?"

"Oh, sure," said Sarah. "Long as you give me time."

"I'll help," said Benjie.

"What d'you want them for?" asked Hugh, looking doubtful.

"Well there's Rafael over the street and José round

the corner and Carlito on Seventy-ninth. . . . I could get them to pin them up on *their* bulletin boards. . . ."

"Other doormen, these?" asked Peter.

"Yeah . . . And then I could get some pinned up in some of the bars around here, where you wouldn't know, but where some of the guys who just hang around all day will see them. *They'd* be interested," said Pepe, tapping the twenty-dollar part of the notice with a plump, yellow finger.

"Gee, thanks, Pepe!" said Hugh. "Give him the lot, Sarah. We'll run some more off."

"When you do," said Pepe, "take some round to the garages. These car jockeys do a lotta sitting around during the day. *They'd* be likely to see any cat straying around."

Not everyone they encountered that evening was as helpful as Pepe.

Starting in the basement, where the occupants' cars were garaged, they soon ran into trouble.

"Who-who's there?" asked a woman, who'd come down to get a parcel she'd left in her trunk, just as the search was getting under way.

It was dimly lit down there and the note of fear in her voice was understandable. For the children were on their hands and knees, peering under the cars. All she could see of them was a strange flashing among the shadows at floor level—a flashing that seemed connected in some way with the eerie sounds she'd heard on entering the basement: a crinkly, tinkling, grating noise; a steady rhythmic rattle as of metal on porce-

lain; a grunting; and a hoarse whispering of the word
"Manhattan" that was so unexpected that it sent
shivers down her back.

Gangsters fixing a time bomb under someone's car?
The lady had been reading about the Mafia and was
more than ready to put the crinkling sound down to
that.

Or invaders from outer space—spindly, horrible
robots with steel fingers and porcelain joints that in-
sulated their own bodies from the high-voltage charges
they could emit from their fingertips? She was a great
science-fiction enthusiast and was quite prepared to
put the rattle down to *that*.

Or foreign agents, transmitting messages back to
their native land, giving their bearings with that one
whispered, continually repeated word, "Manhattan"?
She read her newspapers and was only too ready to
believe that, as well.

No wonder her voice quavered as she asked who
was there. No wonder she gave a long, piercing scream
when, as if in reply, she felt a hand clutch the hem of
her skirt at the back.

It was only Sarah, just getting up from her hands
and knees at the side of the Cadillac next to which
the woman had been standing. And it wasn't as if
Sarah had been deliberately trying to scare the woman.
As she tried to explain: "I—I slipped on some oil or
something. I'm sorry, ma'am."

"We were only looking for a cat, ma'am," explained
Hugh, rising from his cluster of shadows.

"Have you seen one? A Siamese?" asked Benjie.

"Called Manhattan?" added Peter.

Even then the woman wasn't sure. She was new to the apartment building herself and didn't recognize any of them. Children were one thing, she told herself. But children lurking in a dimly lit garage at night, holding combs and saucers and forks and brushes and a sinister wicker basket, were something else again.

Maybe they weren't children at all. Maybe this was a coven of witches, interrupted in some horrible rite, who'd rapidly turned themselves into children to disarm suspicion. The girl looked very old-fashioned, very knowing, as she stared gravely up. And two of the boys spoke with very peculiar accents. And what was that other boy doing, dangling a paper butterfly or moth or bat on a piece of grimy string?

"Don't you come a step nearer with that!" she croaked. Then: "Oh, thank heavens you've come!" she cried, as Pepe burst into the basement, night stick raised at the ready, in answer to her first scream.

Whereupon she fainted, nearly crushing Hugh against the side of the Cadillac.

They were careful after that to post sentinels wherever they paused to rattle the fork on the saucer or rustle the toys or run the steel comb through the brushes or dash the bristles against the side of the bowl. Usually it was Benjie and Sarah who stood guard, ready to explain to anyone who came along what their brothers were doing, acting in this strange way at the side of ventilator shafts, or outside empty apartments, or on the landings of the emergency stairs.

Sometimes the people so warned were very sympathetic, cat lovers themselves, who promised to keep a special lookout for Manhattan. Sometimes they looked at the children suspiciously, as if sensing a mischief that this searching was only a cover for. Once it was a mixture—a cat lover who was also suspicious. Her own cat had been attracted to the door by the fork rattling in the corridor and she had thought for a while that they were cat stealers rather than cat seekers.

And there were several cat haters. One, a red-haired man, told them to beat it—making their noise and disturbing his beagle. Another man, very old, with white hair and thin freckled hands, started trembling at the very mention of the word "cat," saying he couldn't stand them, no sir, never had, and couldn't understand why the management didn't ban them. And a woman who found them rechecking one of the laundry rooms said:

"Cat? What cat? Where?"

"We were just checking to see if it hasn't gotten into the washing machine, ma'am."

The woman's lips twitched in a thin smile.

"You know what?" she said. "If it had of—and I'd of found it—I'd of filled up with water and switched on!"

"What a horrible woman!" Sarah said afterward.

"I'd put *her* in and switch on if she did!" growled Benjie.

"Surely she didn't mean it?" said Peter.

"I wouldn't like to bet on it," said Hugh. "There are some queer characters around."

Peter thought of that as he lay awake in bed that night. And once he'd thought about it again he couldn't get it out of his mind. What Hugh had said was right. He remembered reading in the newspapers back home cases of cruelty to animals that had made him cry and have nightmares for weeks afterward.

Wherever she was—and Peter was convinced that the cat was still alive, possibly wounded, certainly frightened—there were some backs she'd better not jump on, some thin lips she'd better not answer to, some hard, clutching hands she'd better not fall into. . . .

He lay awake a long time.

13

"There's a Cat in There!"

The next day began quietly enough. The river was a silvery blue under a clear sky and the opposite bank had only a slight haze to mask its details. Up toward the bridge, Benjie could see sandy cliffs and trees and all at once it looked inviting.

"Boats go up there," he said. "Trip boats. Look, there's one going past now. . . . Why don't *we* go on a trip up the river? Chico was saying you can go for a whole day, stopping off for a picnic. He said Rip Van Winkle used to live up there and there's a prison and—"

"And all right, we'll go up there. We'll go on one of these trips. One day. Soon. When we've found Manhattan."

It was shortly after breakfast. Peter and Benjie were out on the balcony waiting for Hugh's silently communicated signal to say that his mother had gone out to the dentist (a hand in the air, a clenched fist, a jerk downward) and that it was all clear for the meeting to be held in the Brodie apartment (both arms swung out sideways, with fingers drooping downward, and swung back again with fingers wriggling).

"What is this stupid meeting about anyway?" asked Benjie, having noticed the direction of his brother's glances.

"I don't know for sure. He calls it a Catnet Conference—that's what he said over the phone anyway. And he's inviting some other kids."

"You mean he's getting some others to help?"

"I think so—yes."

"Well in that case we can have a day off and go up the river on a—"

"In that case we can*not!* This is our cat, remember, and—huh! there he is now."

Seven floors below and to the right, the upturned

round face of Hugh appeared. An arm reached up, made a fist, jerked down. Two arms were then spread out, palms down, fingers drooping. They came together again, fingers wriggling. And, on various balconies up and down the building, others, including Peter, returned the message: "We're on our way." (Arm extended, palm vertical—then three chopping movements. More or less.)

"So I want you guys to study this carefully."

With a ruler, Hugh Brodie tapped the map of Manhattan he'd pinned to the wall behind his bed. The others crowded closer: Peter; Benjie (now looking completely alert, his trip upriver forgotten); Hugh's friend Carl; a pair of twin boys about ten years old, with ginger hair, whose names Peter hadn't been able to catch; a fat girl with long brown hair called Grace, a bit older than Peter and many pounds heavier; and three Chinese-American brothers about six, eleven, and thirteen years old called Franklin, Foster, and Fitzgerald.

"You'll see I've drawn a red line running across north of here, then down along the—er—"

"East," said Fitzgerald, the oldest of the Chinese-Americans.

"North to south along the east, and then across toward the river again, south of here."

"So?" said Carl.

"So it's around those red lines you've got to concentrate."

"Why?" asked Grace, smiling at Carl and smoothing her hair.

"Because," explained Hugh, "they're roughly a quarter of a mile away from here."

"*Very* roughly," said Fitzgerald. "The line should be circular if every part of it—"

"I know, I know!" snapped Hugh. "But marking it by streets is more—more—"

"Practical," said Fitzgerald. "Yeah. I guess he's right," he said to his brothers, who'd been watching him with unblinking, serious eyes, as if waiting for his verdict. "Go on."

"Thank you," said Hugh. "Thank you very much for permitting me to go on with my conference, in *my* apartment. . . ."

Fitzgerald was shrugging.

"If that's the way you feel . . ."

He turned to go. Foster and Franklin turned with him.

"I'm sorry," said Hugh. "Come back, please."

Fitzgerald returned to the map, Foster and Franklin at his side.

"Let's just say along Eighty-fifth to the north," continued Hugh, "as far as Amsterdam—"

"That's a long way," said Benjie. "That's in Holland."

The twins began to laugh.

"Shaddap!" shouted Hugh, brandishing the ruler.

"And you too!" said Peter, glaring at Benjie. "You know very well where he means."

"As far as Amsterdam *Avenue*," continued Hugh. "And then down to about Seventy-fifth—"

"'About'? Can't you be more precise?" asked Fitzgerald. Foster and Franklin nodded their blue-black heads vigorously in agreement.

"Then down to Seventy-fourth then," groaned Hugh. "And in along to the river. The *Hudson* River," he added, with a challenging glare at Fitzgerald and another for Grace, who was making rolling eyes at Carl. "I want you to spread out—Carl, Grace, Rodney and Ricky—" (The twins nodded, their grins freezing.) "—and Fitzgerald, Foster, Franklin . . . I want you to cover those particular streets and the Amsterdam Avenue stretch very carefully—"

"Why there?" asked Carl.

"Yes: why there?" echoed Grace, looking at Carl for approval—in vain.

"Because I've been reading—"

"He can read!" said Rodney, turning to Ricky with mock wonderment.

"This is serious," snapped Hugh.

"Yeah. Shaddap!" said Carl, scowling at the twins. "This is my question he's answering."

"Hoodlums," added Grace. "I'd throw them out."

"Because I've been reading about cats," said Hugh, picking up a book and letting it drop to the bed. "And it says it's a load of hogwash—well, not quite—but it just isn't *true* about them all being so smart at finding their way back home. Some are, sure—but most of them are pretty poor once they get about a quarter of a mile from home."

"Pretty *dumb!*" said Carl, who was more of a dog fancier.

MANHATTAN IS MISSING   141

"*Real* dumb!" said Grace, who (Peter was beginning to suspect) was more of a Carl fancier.

"*Not* so dumb," Hugh corrected them. "Because when they do find they're lost they don't panic and scamper around every which way—"

"Like dopey dogs!" grunted Benjie, giving Carl and Grace a defiant glare.

"Cats are smart enough," went on Hugh, "to lie low. As soon as they realize they're lost. Hole up some-wheres and wait." His face broadened into a wide, proud grin. "So that's why it's important to concentrate here." He ran his ruler along the red line. "Where Manhattan might have done just that."

"Sounds reasonable," said Carl.

"Very reasonable," said Grace.

"When do we start?" asked Fitzgerald.

"Soon," said Hugh. "Soon . . . soon . . . But first—" He picked up a pile of extra notices that Sarah had typed. "I want to give you each some of these."

"Notices," said Sarah, looking all around and smiling. "About the cat. I got up at six this morning—"

"All right, all right, cut the commercial," said Hugh. He began giving them out, half a dozen or so to each person. "I want you to concentrate on these areas, paying special attention to any old empty places—but mainly talking to people, *interviewing* them, asking if they've seen a stray Siamese around in the past twenty-four hours, telling them about the reward, and —if they seem specially interested and intelligent—giving them one of the notices. O.K.?"

They mumbled their O.K.s as they studied the notices themselves.

"O.K.," said Hugh. "Ricky, Rodney—I want you to cover Eighty-fifth in from the river to Amsterdam. Grace—you take the south—Seventy-fourth in from the river. Carl—you'd better do Amsterdam down from Eighty-fifth to about Eightieth, right? And Fitzgerald—"

"We stay together," said the oldest of the three brothers. "Or we don't go at all."

"I know, I know, I know!" said Hugh. "Just let me finish . . . Fitzgerald, Foster, Franklin—you take Amsterdam from about—sorry—from *precisely* Eightieth down to Seventy-fourth. And of course all of you— *listen!*—all of you can vary it a bit, away from the red line, if you hear of any stray Siamese in the vicinity."

"We're not stupid," said Carl.

"What about you—and them?" asked Ricky, nodding toward Peter, Benjie, and Sarah.

"We're going to cover the area inside the red line," said Hugh. "Peter, Benjie, and I. Sarah'll be staying here at Search Headquarters ready to take any calls. The number's the second on these lists. Call in if you turn anything special up."

"What about expenses for calls?" asked Fitzgerald. Foster and Franklin nodded, as if to say, "Yeah? . . . Yeah?"

"You'll get them back," said Hugh.

"And there's always the reward," said Peter.

"Any more questions?" asked Hugh.

"Yes. Why can't I go with Carl?" asked Grace, pouting.

"Because the D.A. says you can't!" said Carl severely. "And what the D.A. says goes, baby."

"I *could* rearrange it," said Hugh, looking rather flattered at Carl's designation.

"Forget it! It's fine the way it is!" growled Carl, rapidly leaving.

Hugh, Peter, and Benjie started in Riverside Park. It wasn't as busy as on the afternoon that Manhattan had been taken there for an outing, but that was all to the good according to Hugh.

"If she is hiding out someplace in here," he said, "she won't be as scared to show herself when she hears us."

They had brought their Basic Equipment with them. Benjie was carrying the basket while Hugh held the fork and saucer at the ready and Peter ran the comb through one of the brushes. In this way—rather like water diviners—they spent nearly an hour prowling around bushes, peering up into trees, and looking into the holes and corners of the brightly painted equipment in the Play Space—where they attracted the attention of a number of curious small children.

"What they lookin' for?" asked one of these.

"Gold," said Benjie. "He's got a fork to scratch the nuggets out of the cracks with and he's got a brush for the gold dust."

The kids crowded closer.

"Don't be a fool, Benjie!" said Peter. "We don't want a gallery following us around."

"Least we don't want 'em looking for something that doesn't exist," said Hugh. "When they might as well be keeping their eyes open for something that does. . . . Hey, you kids! Listen. We're looking for a cat, a Siamese cat. . . . Know what that is?"

The children didn't look quite so interested at the prospect of seeking a mere cat, but they listened carefully enough and scampered away gleefully when Hugh announced that there was a twenty-dollar reward.

"Some of them didn't seem too sure when you described what a Siamese was like," said Peter. "I hope they don't start fetching every cat they see."

"Those stupid enough to do that'll soon get tired," said Hugh. "The others—well—you never know. . . . But come on. Here's a cop. We might as well start asking the sort of people who *will* know a Siamese when they see one."

The policeman who was approaching them on horseback couldn't have been better equipped as far as Hugh's last remark was concerned.

"Well, well, well—risking it again, eh?" he said, leaning forward and nodding at the basket in Benjie's hand.

It was the man whose broad back had lured Manhattan off the tree, three days earlier.

Sadly, Peter explained what had happened and the policeman's grin faded.

"I'll keep a look out for her," he said, folding up the

notice they'd given him and sticking it behind his note-book. "If she shows herself here at all, we'll find her."

"'We'?" said Hugh. "You'll tell the others?"

"Sure," said the policeman. "It's what we're here for . . . And here's one now."

Another policeman approached, this time buzzing along the path on a motor scooter.

"Gee, thanks!" said Hugh.

"You're welcome," said the policeman to Hugh. "Ever been to Liverpool or did I ask already?" he said to Peter. "Hi!" he greeted his colleague. "We got a missing cat query."

"Let's go," said Hugh to the others. "That should take care of the park."

"Why didn't we give Carl and Grace and the others some Base Equipment?" asked Benjie, as they went down to the edge of the river to where the small boats were moored.

"*Basic* Equipment," said Peter. "Because—well, why didn't we?" he asked Hugh. "I didn't think of it."

"I did," said Hugh. "And no. It would have wasted too much time. They've got a lot of ground to cover as it is. And it's better they spend their time asking around."

"It doesn't seem to be doing us much good," said Benjie.

"Not yet, I agree," said Hugh. "But the more people who know about it the better the chances of someone reporting it when they do see her."

The white-coated attendant they spoke to at the

boat basin had been polishing the brasswork on a small
cabin cruiser nearest the entrance and he seemed glad
to break off for a chat—especially when he heard
Peter's voice.

"Blimey, mate, what you doing here?" he asked.
"You from London?"

"Yes, sir. Are you?"

"Naw, Strylian. But I guess we'd better stick together with *these* bandits around."

He winked at Peter and nodded at the other two.

"I'm from London too," said Benjie.

"Well so y'are, sport, so y'are. But *he* ain't!"

"How long have you been here?" asked Hugh, with a business-like edge to his voice.

"Hear that?" said the man, appealing to Peter and Benjie. "Bossin' me around already and they call it the land of the free. Even the kids are bossin' me around."

"He bosses *us* around too," said Benjie.

"We *are* rather busy, sir," said Peter. "We're looking for a lost cat. A Siamese."

"That's why I wanted to know how long you've been here," added Hugh. "Whether you've seen or heard of one straying around in the last twenty-four hours. There's a twenty-dollar reward."

"Ah, is there now?" The man stroked his chin. "Well . . . no . . . And I'd have seen it or heard of it, that's pretty certain. Been here since Monday," he added, spitting overboard.

They gave him a notice and he studied it carefully.

"I'll let yer know," he said. "Count on me . . . But if she's stowed away already . . . Coupla boats left this morning."

"Where to?"

The man shrugged.

"Dunno. But I could find out. Get a message through. Ask 'em if they've a spare hand aboard—female—with chocolate ears and tail. . . ."

"Gee! *Will* you, sir?"

"Sure. Only you stop bossin' these two mates er mine about, eh?"

They thanked him and left, feeling very pleased with themselves.

"That's the river covered," said Hugh. "I'd been worrying about that. . . . What's a Strylian? He sounded English to me."

"Australian!" they told him, laughing, both together, glad to know something that Hugh didn't.

Then they hooked their little fingers, thought of the name of a poet, and wished.

Benjie was gazing at a large pleasure-trip steamer as he did so. Peter was thinking of the cat.

Back in one of the streets near the apartment building, they heard a loud, swishing noise and turned to see a cleaning-department truck slowly sweeping and sprinkling fresh water alongside the curb. It stopped behind a car that shouldn't have been parked on that side. The truck's driver leaned forward on his wheel, bit harder on his gum, and directed a flow of silent curses at the obstacle.

"Lookit!" he said, when the boys came up to the side of the cab. "And they expect ya to keep the joint clean!"

"He'll get a ticket," said Hugh, diplomatically.

"Ticket-schmicket! What'sa use of that to me? I want for him to be out the way!"

He reached for his gear lever.

"Excuse me," said Hugh, rapidly. "But there's a question I want to ask you."

"If it's why we cain't keep the city clean, there's y'answer!" growled the driver.

"No, it's about a cat. A lost cat. If a cat gets run over you'd be likely to come across it, wouldn't you? As likely as anybody?"

Peter and Benjie looked at each other. This was a possibility that everyone had thought about but no one had dared mention. Up to now.

The driver bunched his gum up in his right cheek and examined Hugh with his left eye.

"Sure . . . I guess I do see a few dead cats around . . . sure. . . . There was one this morning. Up in the nineties. . . ."

They stared up at him. The rumble of the traffic, the wail of a siren, the hooting of a ship—Peter heard all these things as he held his breath and watched the man's long lugubrious brown face, with a scar under the eye the shape of a tiny boomerang. He began to wish desperately that Manhattan *had* stowed away on one of those two boats.

"Well," began Hugh, sounding dry all of a sudden. "What kind?"

"What kind's the one you lost?" asked the man. He was speaking gently now, and looking directly at the boys for the first time.

"A—a Siamese . . ."

The driver shook his head. He looked relieved himself.

"Ner . . . This was black. Black all over, save for a white patch over the eyes. Sorry."

"Oh, no need to be sorry, sir!" cried Hugh.

"No, *sir!*" added Benjie.

Only Peter remained silent, thinking about the black cat and wondering whose it had been and whether they knew about it yet.

But he had to admit as they went on their way that it was good news as far as Manhattan was concerned.

"And now we've another pair of eyes on the job," said Hugh.

"Yes, only I hope he'll have nothing to report," grunted Peter, still feeling slightly sick.

In the next street they met the policeman whose job it was to avenge the outrages perpetrated by motorists on their friend the cleaner. He was carrying a bundle of what looked like green baggage labels, and was fixing one under the windshield wiper of a car parked on the wrong side.

"Tickets," whispered Hugh. "Let me do the talking. He might be one of the touchy ones."

The man certainly looked it as he swung around on the boys at Hugh's first question.

"Cats? Cats? What time d'you think I have to be looking for cats?"

"I'm sorry, officer, but—"

"Please, sir, just round there someone's tied one of these to one of the fire things."

Hugh and Peter stared at Benjie just as hard as the policeman was staring.

"Where?" said the policeman. "Show me, son!"

"Round here, sir," said Benjie, beginning to swagger as he led the way.

True enough, around the corner, bright green in the morning sunlight, a parking ticket flapped gaily against the fire hydrant to which it had been tied.

"Why didn't you mention it to us?" asked Peter, as the policeman bent down to unfasten it, muttering something about wise guys and what he wouldn't do to them.

"I didn't know what it was," said Benjie. "Till I saw those in his hand."

"Well that was real observant of you, son," said the officer, straightening up and stuffing the ticket in his pocket and giving the pocket a grim pat. "You sound English."

"Yes, sir."

"Over here on vacation, huh?"

"Yes, sir. We—"

"D'you have this trouble in England? This parking? These wise guys?"

"Well, sir, not *exactly*. Only my dad says that if the police spent half the time on chasing crooks that they do on motorists—"

"He means as they *have* to do on motorists," said Peter, hurriedly.

The policeman nodded glumly.

"Like I said. Wise guys the woild over." Then he grinned at Benjie. "Anyway, thanks for your help, son."

"You're welcome," said Benjie. He took a deep breath. "Is that a real gun?" he asked, pointing at the weapon until he almost touched the butt.

"Sure. It's real. Your cops don't carry these, do they?"

"No, sir. May I touch it?"

The policeman clapped a hand over the holster—between the pointing finger and the gun.

"Benjie!" cried Peter.

"You were saying about a cat," said the policeman quickly, looking at Hugh and still shielding the gun.

"Yes," said Hugh. He fetched out one of the notices. "Siamese. Very valuable. Was first noticed missing yesterday around three-thirty in the afternoon . . ."

After that, they made a tour of the local garages, outside every one of which, as Pepe had predicted, there were men sitting on old greasy chairs, waiting for customers. And again it was the same story. None of them had seen a cat like Manhattan straying around, but they'd keep a lookout for her. Some were more sympathetic than others, of course. Some sounded as if they wouldn't have been absolutely sure to recognize a Siamese cat if they saw one. But they were all extremely interested in the last line of the notice—about the reward—and it was comforting to know that the watch for Manhattan was going to be kept up by men in such good, strategic positions.

Only in one case did the boys come away feeling slightly depressed. They had been talking to an elderly colored man with gray hair and a sad expression. He'd been very sympathetic and had promised to keep his eyes open for the cat. And yes, sure, he knew Siamese all right. He'd owned one himself, some years back. But had they thought of this—that the cat might have stowed away in some automobile? In some top-down convertible, say? Or in an ordinary sedan, come to that, having gotten in through an open window?

"One time we had a cat—here in the garage. Used to like riding up and down, down and up, on the automobiles, on the hoods, in the elevators. Shiny we used to call her because her coat was all glossy black —you never seen such a clean cat as that—and that ain't easy—for a cat to keep clean in a place like this. . . . Anyway, she went missing one day. Looked all over. Asked around. Worried a lot. But no cat. No Shiny. We figured she musta got tired of hanging around the automobiles. Or maybe switched to another garage where they fed her tuna *every* day. She sure liked tuna. . . . Then we kinda forgot her. Till one day, years later, this feller came and said, Did you have a cat here once, black one? And we said, Sure. Shiny . . . And you know what he tell us? That cat had stowed away in his automobile. Yes, sir. He found her all curled up on the floor in back when he got home to Rochester—which is more'n two hundred miles away. And the next day he got word he'd got the job he'd been here to New York to see about, so they called her Lucky and kept her and there she still is, I reckon. . . . Big house, raw beef every day, better than tuna . . . She sure knew what she was doing, that cat, stowing away in a Lincoln Continental!"

As Peter said, gloomily, on their way back: "How do we know *Manhattan* isn't hundreds of miles away? How do we know *she* didn't stow away in a car? Any car, parked anywhere—there's plenty with their windows open just enough for her to squeeze through. . . ."

"It's a possibility," said Hugh. "I'm not saying it isn't. But if we're gonna be put off by every possibility we think of, we might just as well sit around doing nothing."

"I still think she's more likely to have stowed away on a boat if she's stowed anywhere," said Benjie. "Why don't we take one of those trips up the river and keep a lookout?"

"Benjie," said Hugh, "there are possibilities and impossibilities. And there are probabilities and improbabilities. What you've just said is an improbability."

"Yes," said Peter, scowling at his brother. "All you're thinking of is the trip. So shut up!"

"I—"

"Look! What's Carl got?"

They had just turned the corner of the street in time to see Carl, swaggering slightly, go into the apartment building. Under one arm, he had a large carton and, even from where they were standing, they could see the air holes that had been roughly punched in the sides.

Hugh had gone pale. His eyes gleamed behind his glasses as he squeezed Peter's arm.

"It looks like the search is over," he said. "There's a cat in there!"

They ran the rest of the way.

14

The Ransom Note

"You've got her then?"

Hugh, Peter, and Benjie burst into the lobby, where Chico was bending over the carton held by Carl.

"Oh . . . hi!" said Carl, casually, with the same swagger in his voice as he'd had in his walk. "Yeah. Sure I've got her."

"Open up a bit more, eh?" murmured Chico, plucking at one of the flaps.

Carl kept a hand flat on the top.

"Uh-huh!" he grunted. "I don't want for her to jump out till she's safe in the apartment. . . . When do I get my twenty bucks?" he asked Peter.

"When—" The glimpse of the creamy body and a chocolate-colored leg through one of the holes in the side had sent a rush of joy and relief through Peter's veins. "When my dad gets home. . . . It's O.K. now. She can't escape. Open it . . ."

"She's all yours," said Carl, dumping the carton in Peter's arms. "If you lose her again that's your problem. I found her and I claim the reward. And Chico's my witness."

Peter sat down on the bench at the side of the elevators, the box on his knees.

"Be ready to grab her," said Benjie.

"I delivered her. I claim the reward whether she runs away or she don't."

"You'll get your reward," said Hugh. "Only just remember who told you where to look, that's all."

"Well, well—welcome home!" said Peter, slowly lifting the flaps and putting a hand in the box at the same time. He felt the round, furry head shrink a little as he began to scratch between the cat's ears. "She seems quiet enough," he said. "She's probably—"

He stared at the cringing, frightened animal in the box.

"This isn't Manhattan!" he cried.

"Aw, come on!" said Carl. "Don't give me *that!*"

"But it isn't!"

"Are you sure, Peter?"

Hugh himself didn't seem to be.

"The kid's right," said Chico. "That ain't the Cape cat."

"It's a Siamese, ain't it?" asked Carl, with a yelp in his voice. "Chocolate-pointed, ain't it?"

"It's not as big as Manhattan," said Peter. He lifted the cat from the carton. It struggled a little, but he held it firm, pressed close to his chest. Its head came near to his and the damp, warm nose brushed his cheek.

"She's lost weight, that's all," said Carl. "So stop your fooling and get her up to the apartment where she's safe."

"More of Manhattan's tail was brown," said Benjie. "And her eyes were bluer than this cat's. These are more of a gray," added Peter. "And there wasn't a piece out of her left ear, like this."

He pointed to a small triangular nick in the cat's ear. The ear itself felt quite hot. He wondered if the cat were well. He was beginning to feel sorry for her.

"Let me see that," said Chico, bending down.

"She coulda got into a fight or somep'n," said Carl.

"This is an old wound," said Peter. "All healed up— but she seems to be running a temperature."

"Where d'you find it?" asked Hugh.

"In a street just off Amsterdam. Some kids told me she was a stray. They'd been feeding her since yesterday."

"Well you'd better take her back then and ask around. Maybe she isn't a stray at all."

Carl looked horrified at the suggestion.

"But I told you, Hugh—these kids—"

"They could have been wrong."

"But can't we just keep her?" asked Carl. "Can't we substitute her for Manhattan?"

"*Substitute* her!" jeered Hugh. "You take Mr. Cape for a sucker or something? *He'll* know the difference between one cat and another."

"Maybe if we dyed her tail," suggested Benjie.

"And anyway, she's *someone's* cat. *Someone's* going to be worrying about her," said Peter.

"Someone sure *is!*"

There was such a confident note in Chico's voice that they all stared up at him, including the cat.

"It's this ear bit," he said. "I think I know where

you can find the owner. The *true* owner," he added, with a frown for Carl.

"Who, Chico? Where?"

"The lady in 5B—"

"Let's go then!"

"Wait! I ain't finished. The lady in 5B came in from shopping about an hour ago. And she tells me there are *two* notices for Siamese cats in the delicatessen today. Both chocolate-pointed. Could be confusing, I said. No problem really, she said. Because one has a bit missing from one of its ears. I'll call her up now. Make sure." They watched as he pressed the button for 5B. Peter hugged the cat closer, crossing a pair of fingers at the same time. And yes, the lady was certain. The notice had distinctly said there was a small piece missing. The left ear too. She wasn't sure of the address. Somewhere on West End Avenue near Eighty-third, she thought. But why didn't they check?

"You put that cat right back in that box and take her round there," said Chico. "Stop in at the delicatessen and check the address."

"I been walking all morning," said Carl. "Why don't *you* take her?" he added, looking at Hugh and Peter.

"You do that," said Chico, smiling at them. "I forgot to mention. When she told me this morning, she said there was a twenty-bucks reward for this one also."

"O.K.," said Carl, suddenly brisk as he picked up the carton. "Drop her in."

"Why?" said Hugh, nudging Peter. "You're tired, aren't you?"

"I just had a rest," said Carl, laughing.

"But we don't mind taking her."

"Forget it, baby!" said Carl.

"It *might* be Manhattan at that," said Hugh, as Peter very carefully placed her back in the box. "Maybe she did have a fight and get her ear nicked."

"This is a real *old* wound, baby," said Carl. "Come on, boy," he said to Peter. "Stop horsing around and get them flaps down. We got places to go, me and her."

On the way up to Hugh's apartment, Peter couldn't help feeling pleased, despite his disappointment. Some-one was soon going to be overjoyed at getting this other cat back. And, whether they found Manhattan or not, at least one cat and its owner were going to benefit from the search.

Hugh was pleased too.

"This is just what we needed," he said. "Apart from finding Manhattan herself, it couldn't have turned out better. It'll encourage the others to keep trying. I wonder if *they've* had any results yet?"

"Results?" cried Sarah, when he put the same question to her. She waved a note pad that she'd picked up from the telephone table. "Since you went out I've had seven calls. Seven!"

"Eh? What? Who?"

She hugged the note pad to her chest and dodged back from her brother's clutching hands.

"Cool it!" she said. "You left me here to do this duty, so you just cool it while I give my report, Mr. D.A."

There was no arguing with Sarah when she was in

this mood, Hugh's shrug and despairing wave of the outspread hands seemed to suggest. He sat down, telling the other boys to do the same.

"Go ahead then," he said. "We're ready. Let's have your report."

"Well," began Sarah, "there's been a few interesting ones."

"I'll decide that," said Hugh. "The report, Sarah. Let's have the report."

"Aaaarl right!" drawled Sarah. "Call Number One. This was a man. He said he'd seen the notice and he'd also seen the cat. He said he didn't know what chocolate-pointed meant but he could tell it was a Siamese because it had no tail. I thanked him for his interest and said the one we were looking for did have a tail."

"Did you tell him he was thinking of a *Manx* cat?" asked Peter.

"I tried to but he got mad, saying kids these days were too fond of contradicting their elders, and I said I was sorry but, Manx or Siamese, this cat did have a tail. I think I handled him very well considering—"

"The report, the report!" groaned Hugh. "Come on, Sarah. Call Number Two. Please!"

"Well really it's Calls Number Two and Four," said Sarah, calmly referring to her pad. "These were similar, you see. They were both from people—a woman and a boy, I think—saying they were sorry to hear about the cat and they hoped we'd find it. But if we didn't, they had some kittens and they'd be glad to let us have one—or more if we wanted. The boy's were Siamese, partly, and he'd let us have one for ten dollars. The woman's were just ordinary and they were for free. One sounded adorable, really it did—fluffy black with green eyes and—"

"Sarah—you didn't—?"

"I nearly did. Do you think Momma would let us have it?"

"No."

"But—"

"We'll ask her. Meanwhile, the calls, the calls!"

Sarah sighed and turned back to the pad.

"Number Three was a man. A mean one. A grouch. I don't know what he called for except to be mean. He said cats were no better than vermin. He said they carried all sorts of bugs and caused all sorts of accidents. And he was glad we'd lost Manhattan. He said it was a fool name, anyway. A fool name for a fool animal. He got meaner than ever when I told him to get lost—"

"Sarah! You didn't!"

Hugh looked horrified.

Benjie cackled with glee.

"Good for you, girl! I wish I'd been here. I'd have said—"

"Benjie, be quiet," said Peter. "Go on, Sarah."

"So then I hung up."

"So?"

Hugh was looking impatient again.

Sarah looked at her pad.

"Well now . . . I've told you about Number Four. That was the boy, by the way. At least he sounded like a boy, but—"

"But never mind the trimmings, girl. Call Number Five."

"Call Number Five came from Fitzgerald."

"Oh?"

Hugh leaned forward. Sarah tightened her grip on the pad.

"He called to say they'd nearly run out of notices and could he count on me doing some more. I said yes."

"But had he anything special? Any clue?"

Sarah shook her head.

"Call Number Six was from a lady who'd taken in a stray Siamese cat—"

"What? Go on!"

Now Peter was leaning forward.

"Three months ago," continued Sarah, sadly. "I know how you feel, Peter. I felt just like that myself when she told me how long she'd had it. Anyway she said she was ready to bring it around, but it would break her heart, she'd grown to love it so. It was part tabby by the way."

"You told her it wasn't the one?" said Peter anxiously, his eyes blurring a little.

"Yah! You're crying!" jeered Benjie.

"Sure I did," said Sarah, who looked a little moist about the eyes herself. "She was glad."

Hugh sniffed impatiently.

"What is this? One of these afternoon serials? Never mind the weepy bits, girl—the calls. Number Seven. I guess you've kept the best till the last as usual."

Sarah shrugged.

"Not particularly. I've done them in order, that's all. In fact Number Seven was only Rodney. He called to complain that Ricky had made a paper airplane out of one of the notices. He said he was going to put Ricky on the telephone and would I bawl him out."

"And did you?" asked Benjie, eagerly.

"I hadn't time," said Sarah. "I'd just started and he told *me* to get lost. Then he hung up."

This seemed to amuse Benjie almost as much as Call Number Three. But Peter and Hugh looked glum.

"So that's it," said Hugh.

"We'll just have to go on waiting now, I suppose," said Peter.

"Oh, and then I made a call myself," said Sarah.

Nobody took any notice.

"*I said I made a call myself!*" the girl repeated, in a louder voice.

They looked at her. She was looking pleased with herself.

"Go on then," said Hugh. "What? Where?"

"To somewhere we should have thought of right at the beginning. Where they're always getting reports about stray cats. I just remembered and I called them."

"Who?" asked Peter.

"Oh I know!" groaned Hugh, hanging his head and giving his ears a savage rubbing. "She's right. I know where she means. Don't tell me," he said, looking up at his sister, who was now smiling broadly. "It's—"

"The ASPCA," she said, cutting in on her brother with cruel precision.

"Of course!" cried Peter.

"She means the *RSPCA!*" said Benjie. "The Royal Society for the Prevention of Cruelty to Animals."

"This," said Sarah, "is the United States. A republic. The *American* Society for the Prevention of Cruelty to Animals, if you don't mind!"

"Same thing though," said Peter. "Why didn't we think of them?"

"Go on," said Hugh. "The call. Any luck?"

"Well, in a way, yes. They get all sorts of strays reported. And dead animals. But no Siamese like Manhattan in the past week. The minute they do, though— *if* they do—they'll call us here."

"Good!" murmured Hugh. "Good work, Sarah. I'd have thought of it myself before long. But you did well."

Sarah's eyes widened and flashed. She threw her note pad and pencil in the air, not caring where they landed.

"Big, *big* deal!" she said. "Well I don't think you *would* have thought of it then!"

Peter got up.

"Come on, Benjie. We'd better see about some lunch."

They left Hugh and Sarah to fight it out.

But it wasn't hunger alone that had caused Peter to make the move. The notices had quoted their own telephone number as well as the Brodies'. Maybe they'd had some calls too. Maybe one of these had been luckier than the ones Sarah had taken. Maybe even now Adam had the news they'd all been yearning for.

But Adam wasn't in and the apartment was locked. And by the time Benjie had brought the key from Chico, Peter was patiently consoling himself with the thought that anyone who hadn't had a reply from their number would surely have tried the other.

"I wonder if anyone will call while we're having lunch?" he said, opening the door. "I hope—"

Then he stopped and, frowning, picked up the large folded sheet of paper from the floor.

"What is it?" asked Benjie, coming to his brother's side to see what was making Peter gasp.

"Someone *has* called!" said Peter. "Personally. With news of Manhattan. It's—look!—it's a *ransom* note!"

15

"We've Got to Take a Chance!"

"That's the strangest note *I've* ever seen!" said Sarah.

"Me too," said Benjie.

"Don't touch it!" snapped Hugh.

The brother and sister had come up immediately on getting Peter's call. The note lay spread out on Mr. Cape's dining table.

"I'm afraid we've both been handling it," said Peter.

They were all sitting around the note as if it were some kind of dish they were expected to eat—a dish about which they had serious doubts. For Sarah's comment was understandable. It was the strangest note *any* of them had seen.

It was so big. Spread out, as it now was, it covered the whole of the center of the table: a sheet of grubby, wrinkled, and creased, white wrapping paper onto which had been pasted printed words and letters and parts of words of many different types and sizes.

"That's why it is so big," Hugh had said, as soon as he'd seen it. "You can't do a paste-up job like that on an ordinary post card."

"It must have taken them all this time to piece it together," Peter had commented.

"Why didn't they just write it?" was Benjie's contribution.

"Because they didn't want their handwriting to be recognized," said Sarah. "Kidnapers always do this."

"They could have typed it," said Benjie.

"Experts can tell which machine it's been done on," said Hugh. "Be quiet. I'm studying it."

So they gazed at the note for a while, in a silence broken only by the noises outside and an occasional grunt or sigh from one of the four. It read:

> WE have *MANHATTAN*, she *is* safe and WELL, but IF you don't PAY US $200 on SATURDAY we will KILL her & send NEWS to Mr. cAPE at NICE with TAil to prove it, PUT *MONEY* in SEAled envelope & carry IT in fOLDed NEW YORK *TIMES* and WEare SUNglasses and YEllow SHIRT, just 1 of

YOU, and BE on FRONT steps Metropolitan
Museum 3 from Bottom on EXTREMIST left
Going UP, 3:30 *PM* exact TIME, *agent* will
collect, DO NOT INTER*fear* with him OR
folLOW or cat DOOMED

"Mostly headlines he's used," murmured Peter, pres-
ently.
"Quicker," said Hugh.
"He can't spell 'interfere,'" said Sarah.
"Maybe not. Or maybe just convenient," said Hugh.
"*Inter* comes from one headline, *fear* from another.
Same with a few of the others."
"But who sent it?" said Benjie.
"Ah, that's what I'm trying to figure," said Hugh.
"D'you think you know?" asked Peter.
Hugh shook his head.
"Not yet, anyway . . . But . . ."
"But what?"
"Do you think it's genuine?" asked Sarah. "It could
be someone playing a joke."
"Some joke!" said Benjie.
"Or someone who's seen one of the notices," pursued
Sarah, now getting quite wide eyed at the villainy she
was imagining. "Someone who wants to trick you into
paying the money."
Hugh was shaking his head, still staring hard at the
note.
"Could be, I suppose . . ."
Peter was still watching him.
"But *what*, Hugh?" he urged.

"Mm?"

Hugh looked up, blinking.

"You said you didn't know who might have written it, *but* . . ."

"Yes. Well . . . It's someone who knows something about the setup, that's for sure. Someone who knows more than what's been given on the notices."

"Mr. Cape's address?"

"Yes. That's one thing. That *is* where he's gone, isn't it? Nice, France?"

Peter nodded.

"Course, quite a lot of people might know besides us . . . The people he works with. People in shops. People like that . . . As well as other people here, in the building."

Hugh was staring hard at the note again.

"I wonder if someone's done it for spite," said Sarah. "Someone he works with."

"Where does he work?" asked Benjie, looking around.

Peter shook his head. Sarah shrugged. Hugh went on staring at the note.

"We'll have to find that out," Peter said. "When—" He sighed heavily. "When Dad gets home."

"Oh gosh, yes!" groaned Benjie. "There's that. He'll do his nut!"

"You know . . ." Hugh spoke slowly, still staring at the note, as if in a trance. "You could almost make a puzzle out of this."

"Isn't it a puzzle as it is?" asked Sarah, tartly.

"How many newspaper and magazine titles? That

sort of thing." Hugh was still staring, still speaking slowly. "I don't know where he got *Manhattan* from—the word—but that *Saturday* comes from one of the inside pages of the *Saturday Evening Post.* And the New York *Times* is clipped straight *from* the New York *Times.* And the *Metropolitan Museum* bit is from one of their catalogs . . ."

Peter grunted.

"Look, Hugh, this is serious! What shall we *do?* We haven't time for word games."

"And I have a pretty good idea where that NEWS came from. That browny color. The fancy blobs . . ." So Hugh droned on. "It came from a copy of JUNIOR NEWS—that new paper they're giving out in schools."

"Hugh, I could shake you sometimes," said Sarah. "Can't you see Peter's worried? This—"

"Which helps to prove something, anyway," said Hugh, still staring at the note.

"What?" asked Benjie.

"That whoever sent it is a kid."

Sarah snorted.

"Just because some of it's been cut from *Junior News!* Why can't an adult have cut it from there?"

Hugh bunched his lips.

"It *could* have been. But it's not on sale on the stands. It's sold only in schools."

"It could be a teacher then!" cried Benjie.

"Shut up!" said Peter. "Go on, Hugh."

"Well, as I say, it doesn't prove it right out. But it *helps* to prove it's a kid."

"Helps? Is there something else?"

Hugh was nodding.

"Yeah!" he said. He tapped the note, just above the mention of money. "This! . . . It's not enough."

"Not enough?" cried Sarah.

"Not *enough?*" echoed Peter.

"'Not enough,' he says!" jeered Benjie.

Hugh blinked.

"No. Seriously. If it was an adult—and an adult who knows something about the setup, remember—he'd ask for a lot more. Why, I bet Mr. Cape would pay a thousand bucks at *least* to get that cat back. . . . Don't you think so, from what you've seen and heard of him?"

"Yes," said Peter. "I do. But—"

"And that's another thing. Anyone out to make money, real money—some adult who knows where it's at—why, he'd send the ransom note to Mr. Cape himself, wouldn't he? . . . No." Hugh got up and walked to the balcony window and back. "It's a kid, I tell you. Someone who thinks two hundred dollars *is* a lot of cash. Someone who doesn't realize he could get five times as much."

"A kid . . ." said Peter, thinking hard.

"A kid who knows about the setup here," said Sarah.

"Someone—someone we *know?*" said Benjie, dropping his voice and looking around as if he expected the kidnaper to be lurking in the very apartment.

Hugh nodded.

"Maybe," he said.

Peter chewed his lip. It seemed very likely, the way Hugh put it. And yet, as he cast his mind over the apartment children he knew—Carl, Fitzgerald, Grace, and the others—he just couldn't believe that any one of them could have done this thing.

Benjie wasn't so hesitant.

"Carl!" he said firmly. "That's who it is!"

Hugh looked at him.

"Why? Why Carl?"

"I've just got a feeling."

"Well forget it," said Hugh. "I know Carl . . . You might as well accuse your brother Adam."

"Wow! Yes!" cried Benjie. "I'd forgotten about him! You're right! Adam!"

"You're stupid!" said Peter. "And you ought to be ashamed of yourself. In fact I've a good mind to make you apologize to Adam when he comes in."

"Apologize nothing!" cried Hugh. "You don't even *mention* this to Adam, understand? You mention this to Adam and he'll be sure to tell your mother and father!"

"But—aren't we?" asked Peter. "I mean where could *we* get two hundred dollars from—kid stuff though you say it is?"

"You tell them and they'll do one thing—tell the police."

"But isn't that what we'll have to do anyway?"

Hugh shook his head so vigorously his glasses slid down his nose. He flicked them back.

"No," he said. "This may be a kid, but he's cunning. If we call the police, that cat'll be lucky to go on living. . . . Oh, sure, the cops'll probably get him in the end—but it's the cat we want mainly—right? A living cat? All in one piece?"

"Yes . . . only . . ."

"What I'm saying is that we've got a better chance of saving her. . . . We can *pretend* we're gonna pay the ransom. We can pretend your dad is only too willing to pay the two hundred bucks!"

"Which he might be, come to that," said Sarah, looking at Peter inquiringly.

Peter was chewing his lip.

"I don't know. . . . He might—but he might be more likely to call the police—"

"We can't risk that," said Hugh. "And at least there's no use rushing things. We do have until to-morrow, you know."

"And you think we've got to do what it says—or pretend to—be there—take the envelope—then what? What do we use for money?"

"I don't know. I only know that if it *is* a kid we're dealing with—and I'm pretty sure it is—well, we ought to be able to think of something good enough to lick him. Oughtn't we? My brains plus yours? American and English? Allies? . . . We've got to take the chance!"

"*Our* brains plus theirs," added Sarah, quietly.

"I suppose you're right," said Peter, looking at Hugh.

"Sure he is!" cried Benjie. "What do we do next?"

"Just relax," said Hugh. He picked up the note by its edges and carefully folded it. It was so stiff with the paste and the cut-out printing that it made a soft, chuckling noise, causing Peter to shiver. "You have your lunch and we'll be back in about half an hour. I'll go and see Chico before we have ours—and check out if he's seen anyone who might have come snooping around with this."

Again the stiff note seemed to chuckle as he stowed it carefully under his shirt.

16

Hugh Plays It Cool

Mr. and Mrs. Clarke were home early that afternoon. Hugh had called a special conference of what he called his Catnet Team for four o'clock and Peter and Benjie had just dashed back to their own apartment to see if another note had arrived, or if Adam had taken any call about the cat, when in walked their father and mother.

Mr. Clarke was in one of his brisk moods. Not as rare as the slump they had seen him in the previous night, it was unusual enough to pull them up short and make them obey at once when he said:

"Where d'you think you're making off to? Get back and sit down. There's work to be done."

"But, Dad, it's four o'clock already and Hugh said . . ."

Luckily, Peter had done what he'd been told to do *before* putting in his protest. Even so, his voice trailed off at the look he received from behind his father's glinting spectacles.

"Where's Adam?"

"He must be out somewhere. We came back to see if—"

"He *would* be!"

"Now, Bruce," came their mother's voice from the

kitchen, "you told him only yesterday it would be all right to go out for an hour or so now and then."

"He's been out all day practically," said Benjie. "If only he'd been in this morning—hey!"

A nudge from his brother pulled him up sharp.

Mr. Clarke hadn't heard the details. He'd been busy telling his wife to hurry up and join them.

". . . We can have tea later," he said. Then he turned to the boys. "Yes. Adam," he went on. "I'll have a word with that young man when he gets back. Here are your mother and I, postponing an appointment so that we can be back soon and get off to a good start, and *he* chooses to wander about the face of the earth!"

Mr. Clarke slapped the table, making the teacups and saucers rattle. This sign of a return to normality gave Peter the confidence to ask:

"Get off to a good start to *what*, Dad?"

"The weekend," said Mr. Clarke. "A weekend devoted to finding that—that cat. Or at least to finding what's happened to her . . . I presume there's no news yet?"

"Well—no . . . Nothing positive," said Peter.

"Nothing positive we can tell *you*," added Benjie.

Peter could have groaned aloud.

During the early part of the afternoon, Hugh had repeated again and again that they must on no account tell their parents about the note. The cat's life might depend on it, he had warned them. He had seemed so sure of this that Peter, Benjie, and Sarah had questioned him closely, first asking him if he was holding anything back, then accusing him of it, and finally taunting him by saying he was only pretending there was something, just for the sake of play acting.

In all this, Hugh had remained cool, simply repeating his warning.

"Just do as I say," he kept telling them, "and everything will be fine."

Then, maddeningly, he had gone on arranging for the search to continue and the notices to be duplicated and given out, as if nothing had happened and the note had been something in a nightmare.

"It *might* be a hoax," he said once, in answer to their protests. "It just might. So we have to keep on with the search in the ordinary way. With one or two slight differences."

"Like what?"

"Like I'll be letting you know later, at the conference."

And beyond that he would say nothing, apart from reiterating his warning: "Whatever you do, don't let Adam or your mother and father know. It could be just as bad as slitting Manhattan's throat."

It was those last words that Peter remembered now, as he watched his father pounce on Benjie.

"What d'you mean—'Nothing positive we can tell *you*'?"

Benjie had gone scarlet. His mouth was opening and closing like a goldfish's.

"He means there's nothing *positive*, Dad—like I said myself. We know she's *not* been found, and she's *not* been run over or anything—probably not, anyway . . ."

Mr. Clarke was still staring at Benjie as he replied to Peter.

"He said, 'Nothing positive we can tell *you*'—accent on the 'you.' Meaning there *is* something positive. There *has been* something positive. What is it?"

Benjie found his voice.

"Oh, no, no, no, Dad. No. No . . . I didn't mean that—no. No . . . No . . ."

"Don't keep saying 'no,' boy!" roared Mr. Clarke.

"Oh, Bruce . . ." murmured Mrs. Clarke.

"I distinctly heard you put the accent on 'you'!"

"He—he hiccuped," said Peter. "That's all. He's had hiccups all afternoon. Haven't you, Benjie?"

"Yu—hic—yes . . ."

"And when he came to the word 'you' he hiccuped again and it came out louder. That's all. I think it's because he gobbled his lunch, he's always gobbling his lunch, I wish you'd tell him, Mum . . ."

While Peter prattled, Benjie, at first tentatively, then with growing enthusiasm, hicced.

"All right, all right, all right!" Mr. Clarke slapped the table. "I haven't postponed an appointment to hear about minor stomach disorders . . . Now where were we?"

In Peter's mind, the phantom knife began to move away from the ruff of fur under Manhattan's chin.

"You were saying about the search, Dad."

"Ah, yes—well I've been thinking. We'd better inform the RSPCA or whatever they call it here."

"ASPCA—hic—" said Benjie. "Amer—hic—an. Not Royal. This is a republ—hic . . ."

"And it's been done," said Peter. "Taken care of."

"Hm! Good!" Mr. Clarke had been making a list on his way home. Now he ticked off one of the items. "Well, there's the police, too—"

"Done," said Peter. "We've spoken to several. They've all noted it."

"One of them I told about a tick—hic—et!" said Benjie. "A park—hic tick—hic . . ."

"Go and sip a glass of cold water, Benjie," said his mother.

Peter sighed with relief as his brother went into the kitchen. The way Benjie had been hiccing in the last few minutes had looked like rousing his father's suspicions again.

"Hugh and I have been organizing a very thorough search already, Dad," he said. "A really systematic one. We . . ."

As Peter went through the morning's happenings— with the one important exception—Mr. Clarke's eyes widened and his briskness began to fade.

"My word, you *have* been busy!" he said. "Something should turn up as a result of all that."

"Yes. Sure. And now if you don't mind, Dad, we'll get along to Hugh's conference. We're late already . . . Benjie!"

"Yu-hic?" said his brother, poking his head around the kitchen door, a glass of water in his hand.

"Come on. Dad says we can go now . . ."

Out in the corridor he rounded on his brother.

"You fool! You nearly had Manhattan's throat cut then!"

"But—how—hic—what—?"

"And stop that stupid hiccuping," said Peter, shoving his brother into the elevator. "Trust *you* to overdo things!"

"But—hic—I *can't!* I've real—hic got 'em now!"

"Serves you right then!" grumbled Peter.

Sarah opened the door of the apartment.

"It's a good thing Momma isn't in," she said. "They're getting real mad!"

"Sounds like it," said Peter.

Sure enough, it sounded more like an angry mob clamoring for its rights than an orderly conference discussing a search for a missing cat. And when Peter and Benjie entered Hugh's room, it looked as if that boy had gone into hiding—locked himself in a clothes closet, maybe, or taken refuge under the bed—around which the others were crowding, grumbling, shouting . . .

"Who's got it then?"

"Where do they want the money delivered?"

"I don't believe him!"

"Nor I!"

"Nor I!"

"Why not tell the cops then, if it's true?"

"Yes—why not? Carl's right."

"Argh! We're wasting our time!"

"We've been wasting it all day!"

"No . . . No . . . Listen to me . . ."

Like the murmur of a stream at the heart of a whirlwind—a stream that was being ruffled and tossed but continued to flow in the old direction—Hugh's voice came from the bed. And, as Peter pushed to the front, he saw that his friend wasn't under it, after all, but was sitting on the edge, his arms folded, his head on one side, his eyes cast down . . .

"If you won't listen . . . I keep trying to tell you . . . why don't you listen? . . ."

As Hugh murmured on and the others continued their clamor, Peter looked around at them. Obviously, Hugh had announced *something* about the ransom note, as he'd said he would. They looked furious. They still had an inquisitive glint in their eyes, most of them, but it looked as if anger had taken over from curiosity. Fitzgerald was shaking his head sternly with every word he uttered, and Franklin and Foster were also shaking theirs, about half a word behind their brother. Rodney and Ricky had reached the jeering stage. Carl—Carl wasn't quite as noisy as the others. Peter studied him carefully for a few moments. But then Carl wasn't feeling too well, Peter remembered. Carl had been a very sick boy earlier that afternoon. Having collected his reward of twenty dollars somewhere up West End Avenue he had tried to spend the lot on the way back via Broadway. Five hamburgers—was it?—seven bottles of Coke—six ice-cream cones—and the cigar. The cigar had done it, Carl claimed. He wasn't ever going to *look* at a cigar again —ever.

So that accounted for his quietness, Peter decided. As for Grace, she was shouting loud enough, mainly to agree with everything Carl said, but she wasn't

really mad—simply enjoying herself and hoping Carl
would notice how closely she was agreeing with him.

Peter sighed. He'd been half hoping to detect signs
of secret knowledge on at least one of those faces.
He'd been hoping to see evidence of play acting—of
pretending to be puzzled and angry—and the only
person who gave any sign of this was Grace, for obvious reasons which had nothing to do with guilt.

As far as he could see, none of them knew anything about the ransom note other than what Hugh
had chosen to tell them.

"All right! All right!" Carl had clapped a hand to
his forehead. He looked as if the noise was bringing
on his sickness again. "Let him talk. Let him tell us
again. They're all here now. . . ."

Hugh took a deep breath and looked up. The others
quieted down, apart from Grace, who was still saying
that they should let Hugh talk, let him tell them
again . . .

"Shaddap!" said Carl.

"Thank you," said Hugh. "Thanks a lot . . . Now
listen. What I told you is correct. Peter—you check."

"He's in this too!" howled Ricky. "It's a joke!"

"Nothing but a lousy—" began Rodney, suddenly
stopping at the sight of Carl's large, brown fist curling
up in front of his nose.

"Go ahead," said Carl to Hugh.

"Well," said Hugh, speaking as calmly and coolly
as if they'd just filed in in the most sober and orderly
manner imaginable, "there's nothing much to it save
we had this note this morning, just before lunch—"

"Where is it now?" demanded Fitzgerald, quietly but firmly, and looking at Peter.

"I told you—his father's got it," said Hugh, even before Peter could look at him for guidance.

"What's he doing with it?" asked Carl.

"He's going to pay them the two hundred bucks they've asked for—that's what he's doing with it," said Hugh. "The note's got all the instructions on it about where and when to pay."

"Tomorrow afternoon, you said?" asked Fitzgerald.

"Yes."

"Where, though? He ain't said *where!*" cried Ricky.

"No, and I'm not going to," said Hugh.

"Why not?"

"Yeah, why not?"

"Because if I did you'd all be hanging around, pushing your noses in."

"Hear that?" cried Rodney. "We sweat all morning, looking for the cat, pushing our noses into all sorts of dumps, and now he says we might do just that if he tells us where the money's being handed over!"

The mob began to growl again.

"I'm sorry," said Hugh. "But we can't risk it. If the guy who's come to collect thinks there's going to be a crowd, if he just gets wind of it, he'll be scared and won't show himself. And then the cat's . . ."

He passed a finger under his throat in a slitting movement.

"But why not tell the police?" asked Fitzgerald.

"I told you—Mr. Clarke's prepared to pay—"

"He—"

Peter gave Benjie a sharp nudge, chopping short his puzzled protest. Peter thought he could see what Hugh was doing now.

"He'd rather pay than risk even the police getting things gummed up," Hugh was saying, rapidly, with an urgent glance at Benjie.

Fitzgerald nodded slowly.

"That figures," he murmured. "I guess."

"It figures," nodded Franklin.

"It figures," Foster guessed.

The Chinese boys' agreement had a soothing effect on the others.

"So the search is over then?" sighed Grace, casting a wistful look at Carl as she struck out on her own for once.

"Well, no," said Hugh. "We should keep looking, keep inquiring. After all, it *may* be a hoax—*on somebody else's part*," he added, scowling at Rodney and Ricky. "And we can't let it waste our time."

"Well I'm waiting till it's proved one way or the other," said Carl.

"So am I!" said Grace.

"Me too!" said Ricky.

"And me!" said Rodney.

"We've searched enough for one day, anyway," said Fitzgerald.

"O.K.," said Hugh. "Have it your own way . . . But listen . . ." The others, apart from Peter, Benjie, and Sarah, had begun to drift to the door. They stopped and turned. "Don't go blabbing it around, please," Hugh said. "Keep it to yourselves as much as you can."

When the four of them were alone again, Peter turned on Hugh.

"I wish you'd tell us exactly what's going on," he said. "That was a fine way to tell them to keep it quiet—I don't think! You should have sworn them to secrecy or something."

"On the Bible," said Benjie. "Or got them to sign in blood."

"You should have made Grace do something like that anyway," said Sarah. "She'll tell—I know she will!"

"Yes," murmured Hugh. "And so will Rodney and Ricky, if I know them. Fitzgerald and the other two will keep quiet, I'm pretty sure. But Rodney and Ricky—"

He shrugged, smiling. The others gaped.

"Well there you *are!*" said Peter. "You say so yourself!"

"How d'you like that!" groaned Sarah.

"Hugh," said Benjie, as if coming at last to a difficult but definite conclusion, "you're a dope! You're a bigger dope than Adam!"

Despite these strong words, Hugh remained perfectly cool.

"But I *want* them to blab, some of them," he said. "That's what I angled for."

"But why?" asked Sarah.

"So that it'll get back to whoever's got Manhattan.

Reassure them. Let them know—let them *think*—the money's gonna be handed over as stated. So they'll send their agent and their agent won't get too nervous."

Peter chewed his lip. But he was nodding.

"You think it will get back to the kidnapers?"

"Sure," said Hugh. "Why not? He—or they—seem to know quite a bit about what goes on in this building. He—or they—is—or are—"

"Oh, hurry it up!" said Sarah, angrily.

"Well, he's a kid himself—probably. What better way of spreading it around than through these other kids. 'Out of the mouths of babes—'"

"Stop showing off!" cried his sister. "Or I'll scream!"

"I still think he's a dope," said Benjie. "A *much* bigger dope than Adam."

He sounded so confident and so scornful that even Hugh turned to listen to him.

"Why?" asked Peter.

"Because it's all right saying they'll spread it around so the kidnapers'll get to know. So will everyone *else*. So will my *dad!* And if he or Mum gets to know, that cat's as good as dead. You keep saying it yourself!"

Peter started chewing his lip again.

Hugh simply smirked.

"Sure!" he said. "So what? Think I hadn't thought of that or something?"

"Well?" said Peter. "Doesn't that—?"

"If your dad or any other adult in this place gets to hear of it, do you think they'll believe it? Unless

we tell them ourselves and show them the note? All
that stuff about agents and two hundred bucks? Nargh!
They'll just look up from their newspapers and smile
and say, 'Really?' and, 'You don't say, now!' . . . That's
what they'll do. They'll shove it out of their minds
as soon as they hear it—or maybe give a lecture on
rumors and kids' imaginations running away with
them. . . ."

Peter was nodding, smiling.

"You sure know my father!" he sighed.

"I sure know adults—period," said Hugh.

"He's sure in—in—in—" stammered Sarah, with angry
brows but admiring eyes.

"—sufferable . . ." Hugh finished it for her. Then
he jumped up from the bed. "But come on, you guys.
We've some planning to do. Fixing it so the kidnapers'll think everything's going fine is only part of it.
We've got this stake out at the Met to plan and it's
less than twenty-four hours away now, you know. . . .
Benjie—do you have a yellow shirt?"

17

Stake Out at the Met

It was one of those rarely glorious Saturday afternoons in New York City—hot but clear—without any of the heavy, hazy humidity that the English boys found it so difficult to get used to. People were sitting around or strolling everywhere—on the side streets, on the avenues and in Central Park—most of them dressed in light, dazzling colors. It was a perfect day for the writer of the ransom note—or his agent—to pick up the money and then lose himself in the crowded, kaleidoscopic background.

It was a perfect *place* to choose as well, thought Peter, as they approached the long sprawling building of the museum, with its squat, square towers and its shallow domes. For there, on Fifth Avenue, on the edge of the park, it was busier than ever—with people drifting along the sidewalks, taking pictures, eating ice cream—many of them either making for or coming away from the museum's entrances.

"They sure knew what they were doing," said Hugh, pausing outside a sidewalk cafe, where people were drinking and smoking under blue and white awnings and umbrellas, opposite the southern wing of the museum. "This agent could just melt into the crowd as easy as that."

Hugh rubbed a slippery finger against a sweaty thumb.

"Melt is sure the right word, baby!" said Benjie, who had been talking like that ever since he'd put on the big sunglasses that Hugh had lent him. "How's about a Coke and cooling off some?"

His yellow shirt was sticking to him in places. He fanned himself with the folded New York *Times* he'd been clutching.

"Mind the envelope!" said Peter.

He checked the fanning motion and peeped inside the folds. The envelope was still there, fat and bulging, stuffed with Sarah's mistakes: the notices she'd mistyped and rejected.

"Cool it, feller!" said Benjie. "I know what I'm doing!"

Hugh looked at his watch.

"Three-ten," he said. "It's early yet. Let's just walk on a while. Benjie—you drop back. No need to advertise the fact you're with us."

"Thank heaven for that!" said Sarah. "He does look a clown!"

"It's not his fault he's all rigged up like that!" snapped Peter.

He was feeling jumpy already.

They walked on slowly, still on the opposite side of the avenue, unable to resist glancing at the long steps in front of the main entrance as they passed. It was too crowded for them to be able to pick out any individual likely to be the agent. There seemed to be children everywhere . . .

"Keep walking," Hugh murmured, out of the corner of his mouth. "He won't be there first—you can count on that . . . But he might be somewhere around . . . staking out for himself. . . ."

They went on like that for a few blocks until they came to a street corner opposite the museum's northern wing.

"Big place," said Peter.

"Around here," said Hugh.

They stopped near the entrance of an apartment building just around the corner, in the shade. People were strolling here, too, but it was not quite as busy. They waited for Benjie to catch up.

"Keep moving!" whispered Hugh. "Along this street. We're right behind you."

Benjie nodded, adjusted his glasses, and swaggered on in front.

"Halfway along here we're gonna turn back. Do you read me? Fan yourself with the paper if you do. . . ." Benjie gave his New York *Times* a tremendous flourish. "You will continue to the next corner, like we said earlier—turn right, then back down the next street to the museum. Still reading me?" The next flourish caused the paper to flick Benjie's nose, almost knocking the glasses off. "Then you'll take up your station. Extreme left of the third step up. And wait. O.K.?" Benjie fanned with less gusto this time. "O.K.," said Hugh. "You're on your own." Benjie's paper made a last, feeble flicker in front of his nose.

Hugh stopped and bent down to fumble with one of his sneakers. Sarah and Peter stopped with him.

Benjie went on his way—suddenly looking very small and lonely, but still making a brave attempt to swagger.

Hugh got up and led them back to the corner opposite the museum's north wing.

"Three-seventeen," he said. "We'll watch from here awhile. Casually. And remember, both of you: the important thing is not to scare this agent. He'll be all nervy, all set to run while he's collecting the envelope —sure to be. So we just have to let him collect it, move away a few hundred yards so he can relax more and think he's safe—*then* move in on him—when I say. Smooth and easy. You taking his left arm, Peter —me, his right—and you behind, Sarah, ready to grab his hair. O.K.?"

Peter gulped and nodded. Sarah, now looking very pale, also nodded. Then her eyes went wider.

"He's there now!"

Peter jumped.

Even Hugh looked startled.

"Benjie," said Sarah. "Just crossing to the steps. Can't you see his yellow shirt?"

The two boys breathed easier. But once again Peter felt a pang as he watched the thin figure of his brother move through the passers-by and begin to climb the steps. Supposing the kidnapers were *not* juveniles? Supposing some hulking man came along and insisted on taking Benjie along until he'd checked the envelope's contents? Supposing he came in a car—straight out, straight back in, and off—before they had time to raise the alarm, let alone follow?

"Look," he whispered. "I don't think I like this."

"Three twenty-two," was the only answer the grim-faced Hugh made. Then: "Slowly," he said, "slowly we'll just drift down to the next corner, nice and cool. O.K.?"

"Supposing it's not a kid?" said Peter.

"It will be," said Hugh.

"But supposing it's not?"

"I told you. It will be."

"Just because—just because they only asked for two hundred," said Peter. He caught a glimpse of Benjie, behind the drifting crowd. His brother was now standing very stiff and erect at the very end of the third step. "They might be *feeble-minded* adults!"

The very thought, suddenly occurring to him, made him go all cold and clammy around the neck, under his ears.

"There's other evidence, also," said Hugh. "Something you don't know about—yet."

Both Peter and Sarah stared at him.

"Honest?"

"Truly . . ."

"What?"

"No time to explain now. Some checking I did while you were having lunch yesterday."

"But what—?"

"Never mind for now. I'll explain later. Just now we've got to concentrate."

They had reached the next street corner. They moved into the shade again.

"Three twenty-five," said Hugh. "Any sign?"

Peter glanced across. They still weren't quite opposite the main entrance, but now it was much easier
to spot the splash of yellow that was Benjie. For a
moment or two, Peter could almost fancy he'd seen
a trickle of sweat glinting on his brother's forehead.
Then he stiffened as he saw a tall, fair-haired youth
stroll up to the steps on the extreme left, just level
with Benjie—but then pass on. Almost at once a girl
with long hair and dark glasses came *down* the steps
on that side, straight for Benjie—then she too passed
on. Then—

"Hi, Hugh! Hi, Sarah! Who's this?"

Peter nearly fainted with shock at the sound of the greeting behind him.

It was a boy.

A boy about his own age.

A boy in faded blue jeans and a grubby white T shirt.

Him?

Hugh was looking surprised, too—and slightly annoyed.

"Hi, Tony!" he said. He sounded easy enough, but the glance he gave his watch was a bitterly anxious one. "This is Peter Clarke. Staying in the Cape apartment. This is Tony Walsh, Peter—the one I phoned the other day. About Manhattan."

Peter stared, forgetting Benjie for a while. The cleaning lady's boy. Was this—could this be—?

Before Peter could even ask himself the question, the newcomer said:

"Found her yet?"

And at the same time he gave Peter such a look of angry disgust that it made the English boy blink.

Peter remembered how this boy too had been fond of the cat. The look seemed to confirm what everybody had said about him. Tony was mad at him for losing Manhattan. How could *he* be the kidnaper?

Peter turned back to his watch on the museum steps. Still Benjie stood alone. Peter looked at his own watch. The minute hand was just touching the figure six. The time had nearly arrived.

Behind him, Hugh was sounding quite desperate.

"Oh, nothing, Tony . . . just hanging around . . . They—they say there's going to be a parade or something."

"You're a month or two late for the big one."

"No, no . . . not that . . . This is smaller, more private, kind of. What are you doing here?"

"Just been delivering a message for Mom. Apartment on Eighty-fifth. Tell them she can't come on Tuesday. . . . Well, I guess I'll be getting along."

Peter breathed easier. Any second now, any second . . . Then he flinched as Hugh said to the cleaner's boy:

"She comes over this side, then?"

"Yeah . . . yeah . . . sure. Well, I'll—"

"On Eighty-fifth, you say?"

It sounded just as if Hugh was trying to detain the boy, instead of getting rid of him as fast as he could!

Then, in spite of all his tenseness, Peter grinned.

Of course!

If Tony *had* got anything to do with the kidnaping, Hugh wanted to see what would happen at three-thirty. If the boy *was* the agent, well, Benjie wasn't going to be troubled. If the boy *wasn't* the agent— if it had just been a chance encounter—well, here was an extra assistant. One who loved Manhattan, too . . .

He glanced at Tony. The boy was looking uneasy himself, but not a lot. His thin face slipped into a scowl when he saw Peter's glance.

"You sure looked after that cat good, English boy!" he said, viciously.

"But it wasn't—"

Peter stopped. Sarah was gripping his wrist.

"Look! Benjie—and—and—"

Hugh came to his side. They watched.

A boy of about ten or eleven, a boy in a striped shirt, was talking to Benjie.

"Like I said," murmured Hugh. "A kid."

"What *is* this?" asked Tony, behind them.

"Can't tell you all the details now, Tony," said Hugh. "Just stick around. Do what I say . . ."

"Yeah, but—"

"See that kid there—those kids—yellow shirt—blue-and-white stripes—third step up on the left. The stripes kid's come to collect a ransom. From Peter's brother. For Manhattan . . ."

"*What?*"

"Cool it! Just wait for instructions. We're gonna wait till he collects, then move in, nice and—oh *no!*"

A third boy was now striding up to the steps. A boy they knew very well. Followed closely by a girl they knew very well.

"Carl and Grace!" gasped Peter.

"Yes—and there's Fitzgerald and the other two, coming down the steps!" cried Sarah.

"And Rodney and Ricky!" groaned Hugh, moving forward. "Oh, *no!* They must have followed us!"

Even as he moved, Carl was confronting the agent. His hand shot out, clutching at the boy's shoulder.

Then, with a startled roll of the eyes, the boy ducked, dodged, sent Grace flying into a group of bystanders, causing a man to yell and some women to scream—and ran, down Fifth Avenue, in and out of the strollers.

"Come on!" cried Hugh. "He's heading for the park! Let's get after him!"

18

Chase in Central Park

The boy in the blue-and-white shirt had several advantages. He was fast—there was no doubt about that. He was thin, wiry, fairly small—able to weave in and out of the strollers without tripping or losing much speed. He had the initiative—could pick and choose the way he was running. And of course he was alone, able to act and react—run, dodge, weave, decide, change course—much more easily than his pursuers, who at first were bunched close together and so liable to get tangled up with the strollers, the traffic, themselves.

"If only—if only I'd known they were all—all coming along!" gasped Hugh, as they turned into the park. "At least I'd have had them spread out—ready."

"Never mind that now!" said Peter. "We've got to keep after him!"

"He should have kept among the crowds," grunted Tony, just behind them. "Out there. On the avenue. We'll have a better chance in here."

"Yeah?" grumbled Carl, breathing harshly. "Call this deserted?"

There were still plenty of people around in the park—people who stared at the running children with amazement, amusement, annoyance, depending on how

close they came to having their toes trodden on, or
their shirts clutched for support on sharp bends. But
nobody paid any attention to the shouts of "Hold
him!" or "Stop him!" that kept bursting from the leading pursuers. Nobody seemed to realize that this was
something more than a kids' game and, after several
hundred yards, Peter turned to the others and
shouted over his shoulder: "Save your breath! Just
keep going!"

By now the bunch had begun to loosen up and
spread out. Peter himself was in the lead, with Tony
at his heels and Hugh—now very red in the face—
just behind. Carl came next, but he was slowing down
every second, dropping closer to where Fitzgerald was
padding along, steadily, evenly, his face all smooth, his
hair unruffled, his eyes calm but determined, as if
content to reserve his energy so long as the leaders
were keeping the quarry in sight. This was a policy
that, some twenty yards farther back, his brothers
seemed to be carrying out instinctively, except that
they were looking content so long as they kept *him*
in sight.

Next, in a quarreling, noisy gaggle, came Benjie,
Sarah, Rodney and Ricky, and finally—a long, long
way behind everybody—walking a few steps, running
a few, sweating, puffing, but determined not to be
left behind altogether—came Grace. . . .

Occasionally, the pursuers would be joined by dogs.
Yapping with delight—as if this were a special treat
laid on for them by a dog-loving parks commissioner
—they would come scampering alongside, some trailing

their leads, some nipping playfully at flying heels, some leaping up with joyously flapping tongues and wagging tails.

"Get down!" grunted Peter, almost falling over a black Labrador who kept doing this. "Get after *him!* Slow *him* down!"

But the only things that slowed down the boy in the blue-and-white shirt were the things that slowed them all down: the more congested parts of the paths, or picnic parties sprawling out on the grass, or groups of people clustering around amateur musicians, strumming their guitars in the sun, or children playing softball. And, in the less crowded parts, where the pursuers could make faster progress, so could the boy they were chasing.

All the time, they were heading deeper into the heart of the park, where the ground was more rolling and the paths twisted and turned among trees and bushes and rocky outcrops. Here they sometimes lost sight of the boy for several seconds at a time.

"Spread out more!" cried Hugh, during one of these intervals. "For Pete's sake! Or we'll lose him altogether . . . And—and when you see him," added the inventor of Silent Communications, "holler—holler out 'Thar he blows!'—anything!"

By now there were just the three of them: Peter, Hugh, and Tony.

We need a hunting horn, thought Peter, as Hugh dashed off. Then, less than a minute later, from up a grassy hillock to his left—causing another dog to come bounding and barking toward them and a couple of lovers to sit bolt upright, startled—there came Hugh's cry: *"Tha-a-ar he blows!"*

Peter and Tony ran up the hill just in time to see a blue-and-white shirt flash around the edge of some rocks, with Hugh halfway there already, in pursuit. Then, reaching the rocks, once again they found they'd been shaken off. They stared, panting, at a twisting network of paths, winding in and out of bushes and down between more rocks, toward what looked to Peter like a lake, judging from the shimmering pale-blue stretches of water that he could glimpse there.

"Where—where—?"

Anxiously he scanned the paths. People were strolling here, too, but they seemed quite calm, quite undisturbed by any fleeing figure.

"We've lost him!" said Tony—emphatically—sounding resigned to the fact.

"He can't be far away," murmured Hugh.

"He'll be somewhere among the bushes," grunted Peter. "Behind a rock, maybe. Hiding. Resting as well . . ."

"Spread out again," said Hugh. "And don't forget to holler."

Tony shrugged. Peter nodded. Hugh started down the slope, between paths, toward a clump of bushes on their right. Peter took the left-hand side of the hollow and began cautiously to climb toward another outcrop of rocks on the opposite side. Tony followed him.

"He said spread out," Peter reminded the boy.

"No place else to spread to," grunted Tony. "Anyways, we've lost him. He'll be miles away by now."

"Can't be," whispered Peter, crouching at the side of the rocks. "Keep quiet."

He peered around the edge. Again he looked down on a hollow—craggy, with more bushes and paths and glimpses of water. More strollers too, again unconcerned, undisturbed.

"I tell you—" began Tony in a voice loud enough to cause Peter to wave him down angrily.

"Quiet!" he whispered. "I'm not sure, but . . . yes!"

Halfway down the slope there was a clump of bushes denser than the rest. Peter had seen a movement there. At first he thought it might have been a bird, but then he'd caught sight of a patch of blue-and-white cloth.

"He's there!" he whispered to Tony.

Once he had the patch of shirt focused, it was easy to make out more of the crouching figure.

"Where?"

"Down there! In that clump of bushes! Don't shout, though. He's half turned to the right. I think he's watching Hugh. We'll creep down and jump on him, make sure of him."

Cautiously, keeping his eyes on the clump and bending low, Peter began to move toward the crouching figure. And, as he moved closer, he gradually unbent and increased his pace. Still the crouching figure continued to look in the other direction. Peter's heart began to beat faster. He got ready for the final leap, gauging the distance, choosing a likely gap between the branches and leaves. Then:

"Hagh!" he grunted, as a body came hurtling and crashing past him, knocking him off balance.

The crouching boy twisted around, eyes flashing, as Tony went sprawling through the foliage toward him. Then the agent threw himself to one side, wriggled away from the other boy's clutching hands, and darted out of the bushes and away.

"*Thar he blows!*" yelled Peter, getting to his feet. "You fool!" he added. "I'd nearly got him!"

Tony shrugged. It suddenly seemed to Peter that the other was smiling inwardly. He had that look about the eyes. Could it have been that he hated Peter so much he was prepared to risk letting the agent slip away? Was it that he couldn't bear the thought of Peter succeeding even in a task that meant so much to them both? Even though it was Manhattan they were doing this for? Even though it was the cat's life that was at stake . . . ?

All this flashed through Peter's mind as he went after the agent, waving to Hugh to follow them. Then he told himself to concentrate on the chase. He'd been forgetting about the cat in all the excitement. Whatever happened, they had to catch that boy.

Adam Clarke had been finding life very pleasant, that afternoon. The sun was shining, the air was clear, Julie was at his side, and his conscience was untroubled. True, he had promised his father that he would join in the search. True, he was now sitting back in one of the open-air cafes in Central Park, sipping a cool drink, and chatting with the American girl on practically every subject other than missing cats.

But what would people *have* him do? When a lost cat could be anywhere within a radius of five or six miles from home, why choose to search in all the dismal, gloomy places? Manhattan was a Siamese, wasn't she? A luxury cat? A cat of expensive tastes . . . ? Well then, wasn't it only natural that she should select a decent place to get lost in—a well-appointed park offering her all those little extra treats she was normally deprived of, like grass to nibble, and rough-barked trees to sharpen her claws on? There was of course Riverside Park—but the kids had combed that pretty thoroughly and, besides, it was too near the apartment. Adam had a theory that the best way to find any lost living creature—human or animal—was to stay put in a likely place and, in due course, he, she, or it would be sure to amble by. At the same time, he believed in staying put in comfort—preferably with a girl at his side and plenty of good quality refreshment close at hand—and although he could have arranged a picnic in Riverside Park, his parents might have come across him and misunderstood the wisdom of his plan. Better to get right away, to Central Park here, where the chances of disturbance were far less and there were waiters to fetch whatever delicacies you required to sustain you in your vigil.

"And you really did speak to Prince Charles once?" Julie was saying. "*The* Prince Charles?"

"He was as near to me as you are now," said Adam. "Almost. He was walking along—"

But at this point Adam's royal reminiscences were interrupted.

Rudely.

By a small sweating boy in a blue-and-white-striped shirt who'd come twisting and scampering this way and that between the tables, steadying himself against some—including Adam's.

"Hey!" cried Adam, catching his glass and dabbing at the liquid that had slopped over on to his best skin-tight, shell-pink pants. "Look where you're going, can't you?"

"Someone's chasing him," said Julie. "Look out! Hold firm! Here they come!"

She was smiling as she said this. Then, catching the look on Adam's face, she frowned.

"Are you O.K., Adam? What's the matter?"

In answer, Adam lunged out, grabbing the leading pursuer by the shoulder.

"Peter!" he growled. "What *is* this? What goes on?"

"The—the—cat," gasped his brother, trying to shake himself free. "That kid—he—"

"He knows where—where it is!" panted Hugh, coming up to them. "Adam—hu—help us, will you?"

By this time Peter had freed himself and was on his way, after the agent, who was now running across the grass at the edge of the cafe area toward a path and more bushes. Adam looked around and saw some of the other children approaching—Benjie and Carl, who'd had time to catch up after the hide-and-seek among the rocks; Fitzgerald, still plodding impassively; Sarah . . . They were all looking serious, all sweating, all obviously not chasing around for the fun of it.

"Right!" cried Adam. "Leave him to me!"

And off he went.

This time, all the advantages were with the pursuer. Adam may have been on the skinny side and somewhat out of condition. His pants may have been a trifle too tight for him to be at his best athletically, and his hair, flying all over his face, a distinct handicap. But basically he was a good runner. And he was coming into the chase fresh. And he was eager to show

off to his new girl friend. And, above all, he saw in this a chance to get into the best of his father's good books. If that boy really did know where the cat was, and Adam was responsible for catching him and restoring the cat and removing the fifteen-hundred-dollar burden from his father's shoulders, it could make a tremendous difference to Adam. Spending money could be doubled. Curfews extended. Bounds stretched to include all kinds of pleasure groves— maybe even a go-go joint or two . . .

The agent didn't have a chance.

"Wow!" gasped Carl, catching up with Peter and Hugh, who had stopped to observe the finish and get a little of their breath back. "Lookit! That your brother?"

Adam was going like a pink-legged, hairy tornado. People were hurrying to get out of his way. The agent was glancing back with a shocked, despairing look on his face. He tried to put on speed but the tornado tore on faster than ever. Only Tony, many yards be- hind, continued to join in the chase. The others were content to watch in a panting, grunting, satisfied bunch. Then up went the cry from them:

"He's got him!"

The boy in the blue-and-white shirt had sunk to the grass, exhausted. Adam was standing over him.

"Come on," said Carl. "Let's hear what he's got to say."

Peter began to move forward with the others. Then he felt someone plucking his shirt. It was Hugh, shak- ing his head.

"That's only the agent," he said. "There's still the boss to catch up with."

"Yes," said Peter, "but this kid'll tell us who that is. And we can't catch *him* till we know . . ."

"I think," said Hugh, "that I know already. This time for sure. Look. Why d'you think Tony Walsh is still running?"

Sure enough, the other boy had gone straight past Adam and the captive and was now mingling with the people on the path.

Peter remembered the episode behind the bushes. "Gosh!" he said. "You're right! Come on!"

Hugh clutched his shirt again.

"Easy!" he said. "I've sweated enough. . . ." He pointed to one of the park's carriage drives, running across behind the cafe. "We'll get a cab. I know where he'll be heading for, and this way we'll get there before him."

"Hey! Where you going?"

Benjie, still clutching the New York *Times*, had turned from the crowd around Adam.

For a moment, Peter was tempted to ignore his brother. Then he remembered how brave the younger boy had been, all alone on the museum steps. He beckoned urgently.

"A ride. Hurry up!"

"To get the cat!" added Hugh. "At *last!*"

"Then I'm coming too!" cried Sarah, who had also turned. "Wait for me!"

19

Showdown in a Slum

Getting a taxi just there wasn't as easy as Hugh had imagined. As the driver who finally took pity on them pointed out, cabs weren't supposed to pick up fares at that point—"but ya look like you're in some kinda trouble and I got kidsa my own, get in."

"We sure will be in trouble," said Hugh, as crisply as if he were in the habit of stepping in and out of cabs every day, "if you don't put some sauce on it."

Then he gave an address at a corner of Columbus Avenue and sat back.

Peter was worried.

"Are you sure we will get there before him now?" he asked.

Hugh nodded.

"Should do," he said. "It's not really been long."

"What I'd like to know is what's happened," said Sarah.

"Me too," said Benjie, turning from his seat beside the driver.

"I'll explain later," said Hugh.

"No, now," said Sarah.

"Yep," said the driver. "Now."

"Oh, I can't start at the beginning!" protested Hugh. "There won't be time—if you *get* us there in time."

"You just take it from where they left off," said the driver. "I'll piece the rest together myself. I'm an expert. I get to know all sorts this way."

"Go on," said Peter. "Never mind him. Did you suspect Tony all along?"

"Well, after a while," said Hugh, "I got to figuring. Who'd be likely to know Mr. Cape's movements?"

"Don't tell me," said the driver. "This is a Mafia plot ya got yourselves mixed up in."

"Who'd be likely to know Mr. Cape's movements," continued Hugh. "Who *could* have gotten access to the apartment and who was also a kid?"

"Tony!" cried Benjie.

"I knew it!" said the driver.

"So I checked with Chico," said Hugh.

"Another mobster," murmured the driver.

"And he said yes, Tony had been in the building yesterday morning," Hugh went on. "He'd been with his mother all the time as far as Chico knew, but he could have slipped away to deliver the note."

"Alibis, alibis," crooned the driver.

"So I was expecting to see him this afternoon," said Hugh. "I was *counting* on it . . . Only I expected him to be collecting the envelope himself, not this other kid."

"A decoy," said the driver. "Obviously."

"And, for a time, I was beginning to think I'd made a mistake. . . . Anyway, we know for sure now. As soon as I saw him keep on running after Adam had jumped on the agent, I knew it for sure."

"And I should have guessed when he knocked me

down behind those bushes," said Peter. "I thought it wasn't an accident, but I thought it was a different reason."

"We can't all have high-powered brains," said the driver.

"But would he really mean to kill Manhattan?" asked Sarah.

That threw the driver. His eyes widened, then narrowed. He had no comment this time.

"No, of course not," Hugh was saying. "He really is fond of that cat, I guess. I suppose he just did it to add to the interest."

"So you really think she's in no danger?" asked Peter.

"Yes," said Hugh. "She's O.K." He leaned forward and looked out of the window. "Only we've got to get there first to make sure he doesn't take her someplace else, and we have to start looking all over again."

"What about the two hundred bucks?" asked Benjie. "Did he really mean that?"

"Maybe it would have been O.K. by him if it had worked," said Hugh. "I don't know. We'll have to see. But my guess is that that was done for the extra interest also."

"Is this his home we're going to?" asked Peter—still not satisfied that Manhattan was out of danger, still unable to rest until he'd seen her again, whole, unharmed, alive.

"Yeah! I'm going to have a talk with his mother. She'll co-operate."

"Well," said the driver, "ya got me licked! This is

the first conversation I ain't been able to bust. And now you're here!"

They got out.

"Manhattan in danger . . . some cat called Tony . . . his mother . . . two hundred bucks," the driver muttered, as he gave Hugh his change. "It don't add up."

"We're CIA agents," said Hugh, giving him back a dime. "Disguised as kids. That's what."

Then, leaving the cabbie to push back his cap and stare after them, Hugh led the way around the corner of the avenue and into a side street.

It was quieter down there than anywhere they'd been that afternoon—quieter and dingier. Even in the still-bright sun there was a gloomy, lifeless look about some of its buildings and, indeed, as the children went farther along they realized that a whole section was boarded up, ready to be demolished.

"There was a big fire here a few months ago," said Hugh, pointing to a gap that was filled with rubble, the remains of old cars, and what looked like tons of empty food cans. "It made some of these other buildings unsafe."

"Those on this side don't look too good either," said Peter.

The sidewalk was cracked and littered with scraps of paper, broken glass, and more empty cans except in one or two places where it had been swept clean, or hosed down with water. A man was busily doing this now outside one of the houses, at the same time sprinkling a bunch of young children, some in swimming trunks, some in shorts. One or two elderly people were sitting on their front steps, watching him blankly. Some other children farther up were chasing one another around the overflowing garbage cans lined up at the curbside.

"Where's he live?" asked Peter. "Do you know exactly?"

"Just along here," said Hugh. "I once came with a message. Before they had a phone . . ." As he walked he glanced around. Then he nodded at the boarded-up buildings. "It's my guess he's got her hidden in there someplace. So his mother won't know."

"Well let's go over there then!" said Benjie.

"No. We'll see her first. Then she'll be ready for him when he gets back. *She'll* make him tell, don't worry. She has her job to think about. She's gonna stand no more fooling from *him!*"

He paused at the top of some steps leading down to a basement apartment. It was one of the cleaner spaces on the street, and the basement windows looked as if they'd been recently washed.

"Don't all crowd around now," he said. "She's likely to get a bit het up. . . . Sarah, Benjie—you wait here at the top."

"But—"

"And keep a lookout for Tony. Peter, you come with me."

Halfway down the steps, Hugh paused again.

"I sure hope she's *in*," he said anxiously, as if the thought had only just occurred to him. Then he leaned forward, peering at the window, and sighed. "Some-one's there, anyway. A man by the look of—"

He stopped. He turned to Peter, his face pale again, perplexed.

"Am I dreaming or is that Chico?"

Peter stared. The man had his back to the window. He was not in uniform and this made it extra difficult for Peter to decide. He was dressed in a dark-blue sport shirt with short sleeves, and he was waving his arms about as if arguing with someone. Then he turned his head slightly and tilted it the way Chico did when he was excited and yes—Chico it was!

Hugh took Peter's arm.

"Just let's step back up there a minute," he said. "This is something we'd better talk about."

"Do you—do you think Chico's in on this in some way? Has *he* got something to do with the kidnap-ing?"

"I don't know," murmured Hugh. "I just don't know. . . . Come on, let's get back up there and—"

"Quick!" came the urgent, rasping whisper through the railings above them. "He's coming now!"

It was Benjie. He was pointing along the street with his New York *Times*—back along the way they had come.

"Easy!" grunted Hugh. "Don't scare him off!"

"I don't think he's noticed us," said Sarah. "Look! He's crossing to the other side."

"Into that gap," murmured Peter.

"And round the back," said Benjie.

"Just as I said." Hugh was looking a little less

perplexed now. "That's where he's got the cat. Come on—let's see if he'll lead us to it. We can talk to his mother later. And Chico . . ."

By the time they had picked their way over the rubble to the back of the boarded-up buildings, there was no sign of Tony.

"Where's he gone?" said Peter.

Hugh looked around.

On one side of them was a high wall, topped with barbed wire, shutting them off from the backs of the buildings in the next street. Tony couldn't have gone that way. And in front of them, sealing off the area at the back of the condemned stretch from the area behind the inhabited buildings farther along the street, there was a huge, rusty tangle of old fire-escape steps that workmen had put up as a temporary fence. If Tony had gone that way, he would still have been wriggling his way through the barrier, or struggling to get over it.

Hugh turned to the backs of the boarded-up buildings.

"He's somewhere inside. Must be."

"But how did he get in so fast?"

The boards on the ground-floor windows and some of the doors were scarred and scrawled all over with chalked names and words. They looked as if they had taken a battering since they'd been nailed in place. But they looked firm enough.

Sarah gave a sudden short scream, causing the others to spin around. She'd clapped a hand to her mouth and was staring with horror at an overturned garbage can.

"I'm sorry!" she said. "It—it was a rat!"

She shuddered.

"Never mind the ones with four legs," said Hugh. "Let's try some of these boards. See if some aren't fixed as firm as they look."

They began prodding and pushing.

Then Benjie gave a muffled shout of triumph.

"Hey! This door! It opens."

They ran to where he was standing. It was one of the doors that looked as if they were in no need of boarding—battered, but solid and heavy. Now it was an inch or two ajar.

Hugh bent to the handle.

"He must have gotten hold of a key from some-place," he said. "Yes. Look."

He pointed to the keyhole. There was a film of oil around its edges, slicking the wood and throwing it into bright contrast with the rest of the grimy surface.

"But he didn't bother to lock himself in, did he?" said Peter. "Why?"

Hugh shrugged.

"That's what we're gonna find out," he murmured, cautiously pushing the door farther open.

The hinges creaked. A faint wave of cooler air, sour-smelling, wafted over their faces.

"I—I'll wait here," said Sarah.

"Yes," said Hugh. "You'd better. You too, Benjie."

"Who *found* the door was open?" growled Benjie, shaking off Hugh's hand.

"Be quiet!" said Peter. "Listen!"

They paused on the threshold, listening, peering into the gloomy passageway, strewn with glass and plaster.

"What is it?" whispered Hugh.

"Footsteps," said Peter. "I'm sure—yes—there!"

They craned forward, listening to the thudding, scampering sound from somewhere in the interior of the building—higher up, it seemed, but getting nearer.

"Someone coming down the stairs," whispered Hugh. "I'm sure of it. Just stay where you are and—"

He stopped and blinked—then turned to the others.

For now there came the distinct sound of more running footsteps and a hoarse shout of "Hold him! He's got the cat!"

"Let me go! Help!"

"Argh!"

After what sounded like a loud grunt of pain, the footsteps continued, and there were more shouts. And then, just as Peter was about to step forward after picking up the first weapon he could lay his hands on—a broken brick—Tony burst into the passageway.

"Quick! Help me! Stop them!" he was crying.

He was clutching a bag. As he came farther into the light, they saw it was one of the small zippered bags given away by airlines.

"Here!" he gasped. "She's in there! Get her out of here, quick!"

He was holding it out. But, just as Peter reached forward to take it, dropping the brick in his anxiety, two more figures rushed into the passageway.

"Not so fast!" snarled one, grabbing Tony by the hair, and pulling him back, bag and all.

Sarah began to scream.

"Shaddap!"

The second figure held up something that looked like an ax. With his companion he was stooping over the bag.

"Stay where you are, all of you, and the cat won't get hurt. . . ."

Tony, who looked as if he'd been about to turn and fight, suddenly went slack. He sat down in the rubbish, slumped, exhausted.

"Do as they say," he groaned. "Please—do as they say!"

"Now you're talking sensible," said the one who'd pulled him back.

He was a boy of about fifteen or sixteen, dark-haired, with a cigarette in the side of his mouth. He cautiously unzippered the bag a little.

"Mind she don't jump out," said his companion, who was still brandishing the ax about two feet over the bag. He was the same age, with a straw hat tipped forward over his forehead.

"Manhattan!" gasped Peter.

There was no mistaking the round head that now came poking through the opening the boy had made in the bag.

"Why don't you hand her over?" said Hugh. "You can't get away with it now."

"Why don't you shut up?" said the boy with the ax. "While we figure what we're gonna do next."

"Yeah!" said his friend. "You're making him nervous. You're making him so he might chop down on the cat before there's any need."

"That's right," said the ax boy, giving the weapon

a flourish that made Peter's legs go weak. "That's putting it perfect, Roberto."

"They mean it," said Tony, with a pleading note in his voice. "Please do just what they say. Please!"

"*You* didn't do just like we said, didja?" growled the boy with the cat, making a vicious sideswipe at Tony that sent his head jerking back.

"I—I'm sorry . . . I . . ."

"What happened, Tony?" asked Hugh.

He had stepped forward a pace or two. Behind his back, he made a warning motion with his hand —a kind of downward waving that was like a miniature version of one of his Silent Communications gestures: the one that meant "Hold it!" or "Wait awhile!" according to circumstances.

"Yeah! Tell the guy what happened, Tony," sneered the boy with the ax. "So *they'll* know not to try crossing us."

"I—*they* made me send the note," murmured Tony, his head down, but out of range of another swipe. "I only took Manhattan—well—for laughs, kind of—just for the night—just to scare you some. . . . I was mad, you see," he burst out, looking up at Peter and Hugh desperately. "I was stupid, but I was good and mad because I thought Mr. Cape shoulda let *me* take care of the cat. Me and Mom . . ."

"Does she know about this?" asked Hugh.

Tony shook his head.

"Nergh! Think *she'd* have agreed? Nergh! . . . That's why I hid Manhattan in here. This was my hide-out—only me and Arthur knew about it—"

"That fink!" snapped the boy with the bag. "Where is he now?"

"Yeah," said his friend, suddenly sounding uneasy. "Where is he?"

"They got him," murmured Tony, flashing an anxious look at the others.

"Who got him? Where?" snarled the ax boy.

Before any of the others could reply, Hugh said: "We did. How else d'you think we knew to come here?"

The two boys relaxed a little. So did Tony.

Peter was frowning.

"You didn't keep her in that bag all the time, did you?"

Tony glanced at him with some of his former hostility.

"What d'you take me for, English boy? . . . I built a proper pen for that cat—with plenty room—ratproof —it took me a week to do it."

"A real pretty pen," jeered the boy with the ax. "It made me and Roberto think we'd come stumbling into a zoo."

"They found it," muttered Tony. "Made me tell them . . ."

"Listen, all of you," said the boy with the bag. "This we're gonna keep just between the seven of us, huh? The eight of us, counting the cat. Me and my buddy here are gonna find her a nice new hiding place for the next coupla days, and in that time you're gonna raise the money. O.K.?"

"But where can *we* get two hundred dollars from?" said Peter.

"Well now, that's your problem," said the boy. He spat out the butt of his cigarette, roughly pushed the cat's head into the bag, and zippered it up. "Just keep the ax waving over it," he cautioned his friend. "And you kids just step aside, nice and easy. And don't try following us. And the cat's gonna be safe." He stood up. "For a coupla days, that is. Till Monday . . . say seven P.M. Yeah, seven P.M."

"But how will we get in touch with you?" asked Peter.

"We got your number. We'll give y'a call from time to time, see how you're making out. . . . Now . . . nice and easy . . ."

They stood aside. Hugh was looking around, breathing heavily.

"Er—just a minute," he said.

The youths stopped—bag poised, ax poised—suspicious.

"Maybe we could manage a hundred bucks."

The youths looked at each other. The one with the bag shook his head.

"Not enough, friend."

"Well—well a hundred and twenty-five . . ."

The boy with the ax tipped back his hat. His eyes glittered greedily.

"Maybe—"

"Maybe nothing!" snarled his companion. "If you can raise a hundred and twenty-five you can raise two hundred."

"Hand over that bag, amigo, or I'll raise a nice big lump on your head!"

The children gasped. The boys spun around, half crouching.

"Chico!" cried Peter.

"And the ax . . . And hurry it up, amigos—you're not dealing with kids now!"

Chico looked taller and leaner than ever, in that doorway. He looked tenser, too, all coiled, springlike, one shoulder up, the other down, ready to lash out with the stick in his hand.

He took the bag in the other hand and held it out behind him. Someone stepped forward outside. They saw a pair of pink-clad legs.

"Adam!" cried Hugh. "What took you so long?"

"He made us fill him up with ice cream and soda pop before he'd talk," grunted Adam.

They caught a glimpse of a blue-and-white shirt.

"It's O.K., Arthur, they're friends!" Tony called out.

"Well, sort of," said Hugh, giving Tony a grim look.

"And *you*," Chico was saying, waving the ax, handle first, at the boy with the hat, "don't I know your old man? *Sure* I do—don't lie. And you also, baby. Ain't I seen you around? *Sure* . . ." His voice rose angrily. "It's hombres like you—" He stopped and spat. "What am I saying? It's *punks* like you that give our people a bad name . . ."

There followed a torrent of Spanish that had the two boys bowing their heads and looking hunted.

"What's he saying?" whispered Sarah.

Her brother smiled.

"My Spanish isn't all that good, but—"

"I'm just telling them what I'm gonna tell their fathers—"

"Please—" gasped the boy called Roberto.

"We only joked," pleaded the boy with the hat.

"Why don't you report us to the cops?" said Roberto.

"Sure!" said Chico. "Sure! You'd like that, wouldn't you? Tell the *haras* and all you'd get would be maybe a warning from some judge. Oh, no, baby! You're gonna get dealt with direct, and I do mean direct. Now beat it! Go someplace quiet and pray. You're gonna need it. . . ."

Outside, they found the rest of the children and Julie there, too: Fitzgerald and his brothers, Rodney and Ricky, Carl, even Grace.

"Two cabloads," said Adam. "We thought we'd better hurry when we heard what Arthur had to say."

Peter was busy stroking and hugging Manhattan. She looked a little thinner and her coat was decidedly grubby—but she seemed healthy enough.

"But how did *you* come to be here?" Hugh asked Chico.

"Aha! I get to know everything in my job," said the doorman, laughing. "As soon as I heard about the note, I figured Tony might have brought it. It didn't sound like the sort of thing he'd do—but I knew he'd been in the building that morning . . . So I thought I'd investigate. . . . Just been to see ya momma about it," he said, turning to Tony. "And, oh baby, when she hears about this I sure wouldn't like to be in *your* pants, either!"

Tony gave a weak smile. He, too, was busy stroking Manhattan.

"Does she *need* to know?" asked Peter.

"Well—maybe not the *whole* story," said Chico.

"I'll get my dad to put in a good word for you, Tony," said Peter.

"And you can tell her the D.A. is dropping the charges," added Hugh.

20

Manhattan Takes the Salute

Cats are strange creatures.

During those last minutes in the condemned building, and on the rubble outside, Manhattan had been very quiet. Possibly it was bewilderment, or fright, or a mixture of both. On the other hand, it could have been sheer, regal speechlessness with rage at the indignities she had been forced to undergo during the last forty-eight hours.

At all events, she soon found her voice when she got back to the apartment. No sooner had the door been closed behind her than she set up a loud, gargling squawl of complaint. What had they been doing to let this happen to her? she seemed to be saying. What sort of attention was this? How dare Mr. Clarke put his great fat face *near* her? she demanded, cuffing his right mustache. As for Mrs. Clarke—surely she, a woman, could have arranged things better than this?

And Mrs. Clarke she flatly refused even to look at, turning her head this way and that to avoid the woman's face.

And where were her dishes? And who'd been eating her food in her absence? Was there another cat? Had they smuggled in a usurper? Just let her get *at* that other cat, that was all! She'd teach them to play a trick like that. . . .

And what about the state she was in? What were they doing—crooning and drooling all over her, when she needed brushing and combing and dusting with powder? And—ggrrritch!—that fly could look out! She'd missed it this time, but as soon as she'd had a rest and a good grooming, she'd snap it up. She'd had practice with flies, just lately—in that stinking place to which they had banished her.

And where was her river, eh? And her balcony? Had they had it all taken away in her absence? Was that it? They'd moved the desk and two of the chairs —she wouldn't have put it past them to tamper with the balcony. . . .

So she prowled and stormed and pounced from room to room, rejecting all their advances at first, licking herself, turning her back, jumping on the piano, chewing angrily at some flowers in a vase, sending Mr. Clarke's best pipe flying off the writing table. She even pretended to protest when Peter picked her up and, with the bowl of brushes and combs, took her out on to the balcony.

But the grooming—ah, it was soothing, soothing. . . . Come on, she squawled. Get on with it! Get that foul dust out of my fur, feller, and look sharp!

Thus her squawls of annoyance turned into squawls of impatience, and impatience gave place to pleasure, and pleasure to contentment. And then at last she purred, happy to be restored, willing to allow Peter to carry her on a triumphant tour of the apartment, to be lifted to the walls and ceilings and the upper shelves of closets, to be reacquainted, sniff by purring sniff, with every piece of furniture, every bed, picture, and ornament. . . .

Meanwhile, as Peter pandered to Manhattan's royal wishes, a great debate was raging among the Clarke family. The motion: *That this house declares the reward money of twenty dollars should go to X . . .*

The identity of X varied considerably, of course—that being the whole point of the debate and the reason for its frequent noisiness. Not that the leading participants in the search and recovery were bothered much on their own account. Peter was rewarded enough simply by having got the cat back safely. Hugh had already made it clear that so long as someone paid the taxi fare and one or two other minor out-of-pocket expenses, the satisfaction of cracking the case was more than enough for him. Sarah, too, was well satisfied, especially when her mother told her that—O.K. then—seeing that she'd helped in such an excellent operation, she *could* telephone the lady with the black kitten again and bring it home, so long as she took good care of it, mind, and didn't leave its welfare to her mother after the first couple of weeks.

Adam, while making it clear he was as rightful a contender as any of the others, pointing out that if he hadn't caught Arthur and got the information out of him that led them to Tony's mother and Chico, the cat might have been taken to another hiding place —Adam then played it very cool indeed. He could sense a great deal of new respect on his father's part

—respect which Adam was still counting on trading in for more time with Julie, later hours, wider bounds —all of which were worth more to him than a mere twenty dollars.

Benjie was perhaps the loudest claimant in the family, insisting that if he hadn't been brave enough to take his stand in a yellow shirt and sunglasses on the steps of the Metropolitan Museum, the whole thing would have fallen through. Outside the family, the most vociferous—and, in everybody else's view—the cheekiest claim was made by young Arthur, who, when he wasn't saving his breath for running, put it to good use in arguing. *He* said that if he'd kept quiet when Adam questioned him, they'd still have been looking for the cat, and if Adam had a case for claiming the reward, his was so much the stronger.

But then there was Chico, and Mrs. Walsh, who had told them where they might find Tony, and Tony himself in a way—for he had known for *sure* just how great was the danger the cat had been in and had suffered accordingly. And there were all the others who had helped . . .

"I mean *everyone* did something as far as I can see," said Mrs. Clarke.

"I know, woman! I know!" thundered Mr. Clarke, beating the table. "But I can't give them *all* twenty dollars apiece, can I?"

Benjie saw it was time to salvage what he could.

"O.K. then—go on—it's a big cheat, but if you let me go on one of those river trips *I'll* be satisfied."

Mr. Clarke stared at him.

Then his eyes lit up and he slapped his hand down hard on the table.

"That's it!" he cried. "A river trip! I'll take you *all* on one. Around the island. Everybody concerned. I'll pay the fares and—er—a limited amount of refreshment."

And that is how, the following afternoon, they all came to board a pleasure boat at Battery Park—Peter, Benjie, Hugh, Sarah, Adam, and Julie, Tony, young Arthur, Chico, Mr. Clarke, Carl, Grace, Fitzgerald, Franklin, Foster, Rodney, Ricky . . . All except Mrs. Clarke, who had a slight headache, and of course Manhattan, whose traveling days, as far as she and the Clarkes were concerned, were over.

Naturally, it cost Mr. Clarke far more than twenty dollars all told, but it was also far less than the ransom money he might have had to pay, and certainly far, far less than the fifteen hundred he might have had to forfeit to Mr. Cape. So he was happy enough, even when it looked as if some of them—notably Carl, Benjie, and young Arthur—looked like consuming more than twenty dollars' worth each in hot dogs, Cokes, and Texas chewie pecan pralines.

It was a pleasant trip. The man with the microphone at the helm, who told them about the places of interest, said he'd never had such an appreciative bunch of passengers. They cheered every landmark he pointed out. They cheered the Statue of Liberty right at the very start. They cheered the Staten Island Ferry. They cheered the Brooklyn Bridge. They cheered the golden roof of the Chrysler Building. They cheered Welfare Island and Gracie Mansion, Yankee Stadium, and the U. S. Veterans' Hospital. . . . But the biggest cheer they raised was on the way back down the west side of Manhattan. . . .

It was Peter who started it. He'd asked his mother to hang a yellow shawl over the balcony railings, so that they could spot the apartment at once as they went past. Then, as they approached the building, he borrowed a pair of field glasses that Hugh had brought along. And yes—there was his mother, sitting on one of the balcony chairs, watching out for them. He took out his handkerchief and, still keeping her focused in the glasses, waved.

"She's standing up!" he cried. "She's seen us! She's waving back! . . . She's . . . she's bending down . . . I think she's going to—yes—*she's holding Manhattan up!*"

Everyone cheered, startling the guide, who hadn't made an announcement for the past five minutes. Then, when the boy with the field glasses said something about a cat, and that she was struggling, the guide turned and said something to the skipper and the skipper grinned and blew the siren—once, twice, three times—and the kids cheered louder.

"She's heard us!" cried Peter. "She's stopped struggling. I can see her ears cupped forward!"

As Mrs. Clarke said afterward, it was almost as if Manhattan knew it was *her* boat—a boat that was sailing past in her honor, giving the royal salute as it went.

E. W. HILDICK, the author of MANHATTAN IS MISSING, was born in Bradford, England, in 1925. He began his working career as a library assistant and later served for two years in the Royal Air Force.

Upon his return from service, he went back to school to prepare for a career in teaching, graduating in 1950 from Leeds Training College. For four years he taught in a boys' secondary school in England, during which time he began to think of writing about young boys. He is now a full-time author with many titles to his credit, and in 1957 he was awarded the Tom Gallon Award for short-story writing. He recently spent a year in the United States as associate editor of *The Kenyon Review.*